"I'm pregnant."

At first, Abby's words didn't register in Dev's mind. How could this happen? This was supposed to be a marriage of convenience. And although Abby hadn't gained any weight, he noticed her hands rested protectively over her stomach.

"Pregnant?" The word tasted metallic and unfamiliar.

"I know this isn't something either of us planned or discussed, but I will take full responsibility for this baby."

Dev didn't know which reality surprised him more—her pregnancy or her calm acceptance of her condition. Abby had been juggling two stay-at-home jobs when they'd met, so she could raise her daughter instead of sending her to day care. He wanted that kind of mother for his sons. His new wife put family first. That's what had drawn him to her in the first place. And somehow they'd get through this, too....

Dear Reader,

This July, Silhouette Romance cordially invites you to a month of marriage stories, based upon *your* favorite themes. There's no need to RSVP; just pick up a book, start reading…and be swept away by romance.

The month kicks off with our Fabulous Fathers title, *And Baby Makes Six,* by talented author Pamela Dalton. Two single parents marry for convenience' sake, only to be surprised to learn they're expecting a baby of their own!

In Natalie Patrick's *Three Kids and a Cowboy,* a woman agrees to stay married to her husband just until he adopts three adorable orphans, but soon finds herself longing to make the arrangement permanent. And the romance continues when a beautiful wedding consultant asks her sexy neighbor to pose as her fiancé in *Just Say I Do* by RITA Award-winning author Lauryn Chandler.

The reasons for weddings keep coming, with a warmly humorous story of amnesia in Vivian Leiber's *The Bewildered Wife;* a new take on the runaway bride theme in *Have Honeymoon, Need Husband* by Robin Wells; and a green card wedding from debut author Elizabeth Harbison in *A Groom for Maggie.*

Here's to your reading enjoyment!

Melissa Senate
Senior Editor
Silhouette Romance

Please address questions and book requests to:
Silhouette Reader Service
U.S.: 3010 Walden Ave., P.O. Box 1325, Buffalo, NY 14269
Canadian: P.O. Box 609, Fort Erie, Ont. L2A 5X3

AND BABY MAKES SIX

Pamela Dalton

Silhouette
ROMANCE™

Published by Silhouette Books

America's Publisher of Contemporary Romance

For Mark, the fabulous father of our children. I love you.

To the memory of my father, Don Gewecke, and my father-in-law, Cliff Johnson, I miss you both.

And

To Chris, Lori, Jodi and Robin. Your friendship and support mean so much.

 SILHOUETTE BOOKS

ISBN 0-373-19234-7

AND BABY MAKES SIX

Printed in U.S.A.

Books by Pamela Dalton

Silhouette Romance

The Prodigal Husband #957
Second Chance at Marriage #1100
And Baby Makes Six #1234

PAMELA DALTON

says, "My teacher's number-one complaint when I was in school was that I was a 'dreamer.' I also liked to tuck a romance novel inside my open history book when I was supposed to be studying. My mother would check on me to make sure I was doing my schoolwork and, alas, could only see the propped open history book.

"My husband claims he taught me everything I know about romance. He's my hero in every sense of the word. My children—Betsy and Peter—are very tolerant of their mother who hears voices in her head and talks to herself.

"I like reading, rock 'n' roll music and Mickey Mouse. I've traveled to Europe—we were in East Germany shortly after the wall came down—to Jamaica and many points in between."

To my sons,

I know it's been a rough five years since your mother packed her bags and left to pursue her career. But there's been food on the table, a good roof over our heads, and we've had each other. For a long time that's all I thought any of us needed. I thought wrong.

With the demands of running my own company, I realize you both need more than I can provide right now. You need a woman's influence. Not just any woman. Not someone who can pack up and leave when the going gets tough. You need someone who will be there when you come home after school and who will stick around no matter what.

I have to admit I wasn't really lookin' forward to having another wife until I met Abby O'Reilly. There's something about her that makes me want to forget about all those painful mistakes I made in the past. She's got a way about her that makes me want to...

Well, never mind that. The good news is Abby has a cute four-year-old daughter. When Abby and I tie the knot, you're getting a new sister and a mother. We're going to be a real family. The five of us. A perfect number. I know I can trust you both to make them feel welcome.

And this time around, I'll keep a tight grip on everything so you won't ever have to go without a mother again.

Make sure you clean up your rooms, put the cap on the toothpaste and teach Hulk a few manners before I get home. I don't want Abby and Paige terrorized the minute they walk through the door.

Love,

Dad

Prologue

The minute Devlin Hamilton slid the gold band onto Abigail O'Reilly's finger, she knew something fundamental had changed between them. Hot desire licked at Abby's nerve endings, taunting and teasing. Startled, she lifted her gaze and met Devlin's intense green eyes.

Did he feel the tremors, too? Did he question the step they had just taken and wonder if they were doing the right thing?

From his set expression, she couldn't tell.

"By the power vested in me, I now pronounce you husband and wife." The preacher closed his little book and beamed at them. "You may kiss the bride, Mr. Hamilton."

Abby tensed as Devlin's face moved toward her. Holding her breath, his mouth touched hers, a mere brushing of lips that released a fleet of butterflies and nearly devastated her self-control.

A smattering of applause broke out from behind them. Trying to regain what little composure she had left,

Abby stepped back and turned to face Devlin's sister and her husband. Gayle and Ed Sutherland were their only attendants and guests.

Gayle, a vivacious woman with dark hair like her brother's, enveloped Abby in an enthusiastic hug. "I hate losing you for a neighbor, but I couldn't be more delighted to have you as my sister-in-law." Then Gayle whirled toward Devlin and kissed him on the cheek. "You chose well this time, brother dear."

From over his sister's head, Devlin invited Abby to share his amusement. Gayle had never made a secret of her support for this marriage even though both Devlin and Abby tried to make it clear to her they were getting married for practical reasons.

The preacher, a slight man with a twinkle in his eyes, interrupted them. "I need a couple of signatures and then I'll be on my way."

Devlin didn't hesitate, he jotted his name with steady confidence on the legal document before offering the pen to Abby.

She tried to quell her nerves and still her shaking hand as she wrote her name next to his. As quickly as she could, she moved away from the charged atmosphere surrounding Devlin. She wasn't sure what was wrong with her. By nature, she was a practical sort of woman who knew the wisdom of keeping both feet on the ground. So why was she so skittish? Why was she sweltering in her silk dress? The room temperature was comfortable despite the frigid late-December chill outdoors.

The preacher pocketed the document and gave them both a handshake. "Best wishes to you both. May your life together be filled with happiness and joy."

As soon as the door closed behind the preacher, Ed

pulled Gayle's coat from the hall closet. "We need to get going, too."

"Can't you stay for a while?" Abby tried to hide her sudden panic at the realization she was about to be left alone with her new husband.

"Sorry." Gayle buttoned up her coat and wrapped her scarf around her neck. "Our baby-sitter has a hot date and we promised her we'd be back as soon as the ceremony was over. But don't worry, I'll bring Paige home around nine o'clock tomorrow morning."

"If she's too much trouble, she can come home tonight." Abby wondered if anyone else noticed the desperation in her voice.

Gayle laughed. "Paige is never any trouble. Besides, she and Sarah have been planning this all week. You wouldn't deprive them of their fun, would you?"

Paige loved to spend the night at the Sutherlands'. And normally Abby didn't mind, but tonight she could have used her four-year-old daughter's incessant chatter to dispel the sensual desire she was feeling.

Instead of coming to Ohio, Devlin's sons had stayed at their grandparents' house in Wisconsin so they could play in their basketball games. Since the boys wouldn't be here, Abby decided Paige could stay at Gayle's. Kids didn't usually like weddings, anyway.

At the door, Gayle turned around. "By the way, there's champagne in the refrigerator." She winked at her brother. "Enjoy."

The cool draft that flowed into the house following their guests' departure didn't lower the temperature of the room one bit.

Avoiding Devlin's gaze, Abby searched for something to straighten or pick up. There wasn't anything. Despite the fact her life had taken a one-hundred-and-eighty-degree turn, nothing in the house had physically changed, including her small and cozily decorated living room.

"Having regrets already?" The sound of Devlin's deep voice made her pulse leap.

"No," she lied, despising her cowardice.

Devlin gave her a quizzical glance but didn't press her. It was too late for regrets, and they both knew it. This temporary, no-fuss marriage was what they both wanted.

She watched him reach for a sheaf of papers sitting on the coffee table.

"I've got your copy of the marriage contract we drew up," he said. "Do you want to review it?"

She shook her head.

She knew the contract word for word. The papers they'd signed before the wedding spelled out in great detail what each wanted and expected.

It wasn't as if this was a real marriage.

Both of them had been burned. Devlin's first wife had divorced him and left him to raise two young sons alone. When Abby's husband died a year ago, he'd left her with a mountain of gambling debts and a young daughter to support.

In essence, Devlin and Abby wanted the same thing: a marriage of convenience that would provide stability for their children. She would be a full-time mother and caretaker. He would be the financial provider.

They'd laid the groundwork.

Neither wanted any surprises.

No insincere protestations of love. No flares of passion that would burn out before their first anniversary. No hidden expectations that would leave one or both of them hungry for things that never could be.

It was ideal for both of them.

Or so it had seemed a month ago when Devlin proposed.

But now, with the gold band firmly anchored on her finger, she wasn't so sure.

What had changed? Why was there so much tension simmering through the room?

Just because she'd never seen Devlin in a formal suit that fit his broad shoulders and lean hips to perfection and made him appear dangerously powerful was no reason to question her own judgment. Or to suddenly realize how much sex appeal he exuded. She had to keep her feet firmly on the ground, her head out of the clouds, and quit imagining things that weren't there.

This was still the same man who'd fixed her roof just a few short months ago. Devlin was a decent man, a hard worker and a committed father. He'd been straightforward about who he was and what he wanted. She'd appreciated that, needed it. That's all she required or expected from him. And vice versa.

They'd agreed they weren't going to risk this marriage by having sex. Sex would only complicate things.

Neither wanted complications. They'd had enough of those with their former spouses. Her daughter needed a home with food on the table. Devlin's sons, thirteen-year-old Jason, and six-year-old Riley, needed a mother.

Abby readily agreed to accept the responsibility. She loved children and looked forward to raising the two boys as her own.

Merging their families was a practical matter.

So why did she have this insane and totally uncharacteristic urge to be impractical?

Why did she want to run her fingers along the edge of Devlin's crisp white collar and release the top button so she could explore the trail of tanned flesh?

It was so unlike her. She'd learned the hard way not to trust emotions. The fickleness of passion could put everyone at risk.

Why wouldn't her hormones behave the way she wanted them to?

Surely she was imagining the waves of desire leaping at her from the depths of his green eyes.

She'd never been a woman with fanciful notions. Love was for those who could afford to be fooled.

Devlin startled her by setting the papers on the table again. "I suppose we could pop open the champagne."

"That's an excellent idea," she said, welcoming the diversion and a way to lighten the atmosphere. She led the way to the small kitchen. "I'll warn you, my selection of glassware is limited. You can choose between Fred or Barney."

His gaze gleamed. "No Wilma glass?"

"It's got a chip in it. I'd hate to have you get cut."

"I'll take my chances." His drawl contained a toe-curling edge.

She stopped and peeked at him out of the corner of her eye, wondering if he was teasing her or if he'd meant something more.

When he asked, "Got a corkscrew?" she decided her imagination had run askew again.

"I never could think straight in panty hose," she muttered aloud and then blushed violently when she heard Devlin chuckle and realized he'd heard her.

"I'll keep that in mind."

"The corkscrew is in the top right-hand drawer." Attempting to cover her embarrassment, she pulled open the cupboard and perched up on tiptoe to reach for the glasses.

Suddenly one of them slipped.

Devlin reached out to her and caught it just in time. His quick movements brought his hard body next to hers. "You okay?"

Turning to thank him, she found herself pressed flat against him, close enough to feel his breath fan her skin. She swallowed. "Thank you. We almost lost Wilma for good that time. I don't let Paige drink out of that glass, but it's still her favorite and she would have been terribly disappointed."

His gaze slipped to her lips. "I wouldn't want that to happen."

"Wouldn't you?" She thought about moving, but her limbs refused to cooperate. A sensual awareness started a slow dance within her.

She didn't breathe as he set the glass on the counter. There was no place to move. Nowhere to escape. His body surrounded hers, and every cell in her body responded to his closeness.

Her gaze darted upward until it met the green fire in his. In the smoldering flames she saw his desire, matching her own.

He claimed her mouth in a long, no-holds-barred kiss.

If she'd thought about protesting or moving away, the option dissolved in a wave of need. She'd never realized a kiss could be intoxicating. Yet champagne had never packed this kind of sizzle to her senses.

She forgot everything but Devlin.

He made sure of it. He demanded it. Impatience made them greedy for each other as her tongue met the call of his.

They found their way to the bedroom, and within seconds, managed to divest each other of their clothes. Then Devlin swept her into his arms and carried her naked to the waiting bed.

"The light—" she started to say.

"Is perfect."

Time lost all meaning. No one else existed. His love-making brought tears to her eyes, amazing her with his patience. Yet when he moved his body over hers, he took her with a fierce aggression that drew her own fiery response.

Devlin made love to her with such sensitivity and passion, she didn't want him ever to stop. He made her feel beautiful.

He made her believe in rainbows, and happily-ever-after.

He made her forget the price of loving too much.

Hours later, Gayle's voice on the other end of the phone dragged Abby down to earth. "Abby, I hate to wake you this early in the morning, but I think Paige has the chicken pox. She's speckled from head to toe."

Panic and guilt accompanied wakefulness. "I'll be right there."

She put down the phone as Devlin flicked the lamp switch. Light flooded the room.

"What's wrong?" he asked.

"Paige is sick." In the face of the bold glare, her nakedness taunted her. She searched for her clothes.

What had she done?

The image of her daughter, cute as a button with a confident, deep-dimpled smile, flashed through her mind. How could she have forgotten Paige and what this marriage meant to her future? How could she have risked everything?

Grabbing the sheet from the bed and avoiding Devlin's eyes, Abby tucked it around her naked body.

"Do you want me to come with you?" he asked.

She shook her head. "There's no need."

"Abby—"

She cut him off before he could say what had to be faced. "We both know this violated our agreement. We made a mistake. Let's just forget it, pretend it never happened and move on from here."

A deafening pause followed her rushed speech.

Not hiding his own nakedness, Devlin rose from the bed. "I'll move into the other bedroom so you can bring Paige in here."

She nodded. "About our contract...?"

"It officially starts now. This won't happen again." He turned away and walked into the bathroom.

Still hugging the sheet, Abby sagged down on the bed. The lump in her throat held back an onslaught of tears.

More than ever she was grateful for the agreement they'd signed. She needed its cold comfort to reassure her nothing had changed between them.

From now on she'd stick to the letter of their bargain and forget this lapse in judgment ever happened. She couldn't let Devlin Hamilton get past her defenses again.

She just couldn't.

Chapter One

Abby's stomach began its familiar pitch-and-roll cadence as she stood in the driveway next to her car and stared at the house in front of her.

With stylish wood siding and two comfortable rockers sitting on an old-fashioned porch, the house was bigger and more beautiful than Devlin had described.

An old longing rose within her. She'd always dreamed of living in such a place. Would this be her real home? Would Devlin want her to share it with him after he learned—

"Mommy, aren't we going inside?" The impatient voice made Abby look down at her blond-haired daughter. Four-year-old Paige, still wearing the soft, rosy-cheeked glow due to a long nap in the car, and clutching her squirming black-and-white-spotted cat who was trying to escape, peered up at her mother with eager blue eyes. "I want Princess to meet my new brothers. Do Jason and Riley like cats?"

The smile came naturally as Abby put an arm around

her daughter's shoulders and gave them a squeeze. Paige was a little nervous and apprehensive about meeting her new brothers for the first time.

Abby was just as nervous. How would the boys react to a new mother? A new sister? If only there'd been more time for them all to meet and get to know each other. "We'll soon find out, won't we?" For Paige's sake, she had to make this marriage work.

Her stomach performed another one of those nasty flip-flops.

Paige tugged on her mother's pants. "Mommy? Princess has to go potty."

Abby knew what that meant. Her daughter was probably the one who needed to use the bathroom. Taking one more fortifying breath, Abby attempted to steady her nerves before braving the unknown. "Okay, honey. Let's go see if anyone is home."

She steered Paige and Princess up the steps and across the sturdy porch. Raising her hand to the door, Abby's knuckles met air instead of wood when the door suddenly swung open and two big, strong hands reached for them.

"Quick, get in here and shut the door!"

She barely had a chance to register her husband's furious green eyes and tight-lipped expression before she found herself unceremoniously yanked into the room along with Paige.

"Shut it, Riley," Devlin ordered.

At his command, a young boy pushed between them as he flung himself against the door.

The resounding bang, accompanied by a whoosh of cold February air, made both Abby and Paige jump.

Paige shifted closer to her mother, and Princess set up a howl at being clenched so tightly in her young mistress's arms.

"Oh, no, she's got a cat," wailed Riley, his bright red hair sticking straight up on top of his head.

The words barely left his mouth when a big wall of brown fur barreled toward them. Instinctively, Abby placed her body between Paige and the hairy charger.

Princess yowled in protest.

Springing free, the cat tore across the room.

The dog took off in pursuit, knocking over the lamp sitting on the end table, as the cat leaped toward the living-room curtains.

"Hulk!" Devlin roared.

The big dog came to an abrupt stop and looked back at Devlin as if to say, "Please."

"Stay." Devlin never took his eyes from the dog. "Jason, grab him and put him in the kitchen."

The thirteen-year-old, the teenage image of his father with dark hair and deep-set green eyes, reluctantly left his hallway observation post. He wrinkled his nose and hooked his hand around Hulk's collar. "Come on, boy!" The dog panted heavily as Jason led him into another room and shut the door.

The dog yelped once and then whined.

Abby looked at Devlin in apology. "I should have warned you. Gayle and Ed gave Paige the cat last weekend as a going-away present, and she hasn't parted with it since. I hope this won't cause too much of a problem."

Jason resumed his former slouch against the doorway. "No problem at all if you don't mind the cat chowing down snakes for an evening snack."

"Jason, put a lid on it." Devlin's expression bore his frustration. He pushed his fingers through his short brown hair and met Abby's gaze. "I'm sorry, Abby, this isn't the welcome I'd planned."

Her stomach refused to settle down properly. "Did he say snakes?"

Jason shot a malicious look at his brother. "Riley's snakes are loose."

Paige's lower lip quivered as she scuttled next to her mother for protection. "Mommy, me and Princess don't like snakes."

Hulk's whimpers turned to a pronounced howl.

"Hulk, shut up!" Devlin yelled over the canine racket. When Paige whimpered in reaction, he lowered his voice a decibel or two. "How was the drive?"

"Fine. The roads between Ohio and Wisconsin are good," Abby replied. Then as Paige tightened her arms, she looked helplessly at Devlin. "I didn't know Riley had snakes."

"We didn't know he had them, either," Devlin said dryly.

Riley's face turned a pained hue of red. "I traded Ben Fix some of my aquarium fish for his snake eggs."

"They're just eggs then?" Abby's tension eased a bit, even though her stomach was still performing a series of acrobatic twists. She had nothing against snakes per se, but living with them was another matter.

"They were." Jason seemed to be the only one in the room enjoying himself. "They're not anymore. Riley checked them this morning and discovered the eggs are now empty. So far, we've found four of the slippery fellas. One in the bathroom, one in Dad's closet and two in the kitchen."

"How many are there supposed to be?" Out of the corner of her eye, Abby saw the cat hook her claws into the curtain and attempt to shimmy up them. She tried to reach for the feline but couldn't move with Paige attached to her.

Devlin snagged the cat halfway up the drape and returned her to Paige's arms. "There were seven of them."

"Seven?" Abby repeated faintly.

Riley looked downright miserable. "Three are still missing."

Paige started to sob in earnest, burying her face deeper into her mother's thigh. "Princess wants to go home, Mommy."

"I thought Paige might like a pet," Riley explained. "I didn't know she had a cat. The snakes won't hurt her. They're not poisonous."

Abby's heart softened at her new stepson's distress as she tried to figure out a way to ease the situation. She hadn't doubted that merging the two families would be a challenge.

But snakes?

It seemed like a bad omen. Especially since she knew this wouldn't be the first surprise they'd have to deal with today.

Unfortunately, turning around and heading out the door wasn't an option. At least not yet.

Not until she could talk to Devlin and explain...

Patting Paige's silky-smooth hair, she said, "It's okay, sweetheart. Riley was trying to make you feel welcome by giving you a present. Wasn't that nice of him?"

Paige raised her head and eyed Riley dubiously. "When are the snakes going away?"

The younger boy's face sagged into an unhappy frown, causing his crop of freckles to march together. "I don't know. I have to find the rest of them first."

"Maybe Hulk ate the other three," Jason drawled. "He's been acting kind of squirrelly today. I bet he pukes them up all over the living-room rug."

Devlin frowned. "Jason, we don't need—"

"Don't move!" Riley squealed, pointing toward an area near Abby's feet. "There's another one."

Abby's stomach lurched, and this time it didn't seem inclined to settle again. "Where's the bathroom?"

Without questioning her, Devlin moved with quick strides across the room and shoved open a door just a few feet from her. "This way."

Abby pushed by him.

"Mommy, don't leave me," Paige screamed, trying to grab on to Abby's sweater.

"Watch out for my snake!" Riley yelled desperately.

Abby couldn't answer, knowing if she opened her mouth she'd lose the battle. Dashing through the doorway, she raced inside.

As she grabbed the sides of the toilet and lowered her head, she heard Devlin say, "Stand back and give her some room."

The roaring hum in her ears and the wretching of her stomach blocked out everything and everyone else as she hung on.

Jason's rude snort broke the stunned silence behind Abby. "Is she going to do that whenever she sees a snake?"

"I didn't know she'd be afraid of snakes." Riley's tone sounded hesitant. "Does this mean I'll have to get rid of all of them?" he asked hesitantly.

Abby breathed deeply, trying to regain her breath and her composure as she rested her head against the cool sink next to the commode. She'd like to believe this humiliation was the worst part of the day. If only she could believe that....

Devlin reached her side and carefully helped Abby to

her feet. "Riley and Jason, take Paige into the other room."

"No," Paige stated adamantly. "I don't want to go with them. Me and Princess want to go home, Mommy. Now." Then she threw herself against Abby's leg again.

The sudden movement knocked Abby into Devlin's arms. He steadied her, and she managed to offer him a weak smile before pulling away. It was important to stand on her own two feet and present some semblance of dignity despite the fact she'd made the most undignified entrance imaginable. "Thank you."

She could see the questions darkening Devlin's eyes and knew the answers couldn't be delayed much longer.

Looking down at Paige, she placed her hands firmly on her daughter's shoulders. "Sweetheart, why don't you go with Riley and Jason and get some water for Princess? I bet she's kind of thirsty."

Paige didn't budge. "What about the snakes?"

"Those snakes won't hurt you. They're more afraid of you than you are of them. Besides, you'll have Jason and Riley with you."

Her daughter didn't look convinced as she first eyed Jason, who wore a sullen expression, and then Riley, who still clutched the small snake that poked his head at her.

Whining and scratching could be heard from behind the kitchen door.

"Riley, go put that snake away and then grab Hulk so he won't jump on Paige." Devlin's voice didn't brook any argument. "Jase, take Paige's hand so she won't be afraid."

"What about her cat?" Jason asked.

"She'll be okay in the living room if you keep Hulk in the kitchen."

Jason's mouth tightened into a teenage scowl, but he

didn't argue. Begrudgingly, he stuck out his hand for Paige.

After a bit of prodding, the three children left the bathroom. A few seconds later, Abby heard the kitchen door open and then close.

Quiet, charged with tension and uncertainty, suddenly reigned in the small room.

Abby tried to swallow the lump in her throat, feeling Devlin's silent questions. She met his gaze. "Could I have a few moments to myself?"

A tic marred the hard set of Devlin's jaw. "I don't think that's a good idea."

She couldn't stop the flush from rouging her cheeks. Lord knew what he thought. With more composure than she was feeling, she shook her head. "I'll be fine. I just need to wash my face and attend to a few personal things."

He didn't move away until he realized that she had no intention of doing anything while he watched her. "I'll be right outside."

That's what she was afraid of. As soon as the door was shut, she released a sigh of relief. She didn't quite trust Devlin not to come tearing back if he thought she was taking too long. One thing she was learning about her new husband, Devlin Hamilton wasn't a patient man.

She looked around the small, yet serviceable, bathroom for a washcloth.

The room didn't contain any fancy toiletry items such as a soap dish, toothbrush holder or even a mirror, signs of a woman's influence. That pleased her more than it should. She knew Devlin had been divorced for at least five years but she wasn't sure how many female friends he'd entertained during that interim. Obviously not anyone recent enough to buy a soap dish for the lone yellow bar that sat on top of its soggy wrapper next to the sink. The only other accessories in the room were a box of white tissues perched on the back of the stool and a roll of toilet paper that scorned the empty circular holder hanging alongside the oak vanity and rested on the edge of the counter.

Before their wedding six weeks ago, Devlin had told her she'd be free to make any changes to the house he'd designed and built two years ago.

But how many changes would he tolerate?

The one she was about to propose wouldn't be what he'd intended. But then it hadn't been part of her game plan, either. Still, she was willing to adjust. Would Devlin?

She forced back her thoughts. Second-guessing her new husband's reaction had been a futile activity she'd indulged in all too frequently lately. The trouble was, they barely knew each other.

They'd married for convenience's sake. Their marriage had seemed the perfect solution for both of them. But six long weeks had come and gone. It was now the middle of February. Nothing had gone according to plan since the moment they'd said "I do."

She had no idea how the future would pan out.

Hearing Devlin's footsteps as he prowled outside the bathroom door, she opened a built-in cabinet next to the sink and discovered a hodgepodge of white washcloths that looked as if they'd been hastily thrown into the cupboard. With a wry smile, she reached in and took one. She was tempted to fold the untidy trove and replace them neatly in the cupboard. Did she have the right to start rearranging?

No. Not yet. Not until after she talked to Devlin.

After running warm water over the cloth, she held it

against her face, putting off the confrontation. Finally, she'd done everything she could to resurrect a little dignity.

Opening the door, she bumped into Devlin's hard-muscled chest.

His callused fingers caressed her arms, reminding her of the last time his hands had touched her. She pushed back the memory and stepped away from him, able to raise her gaze only as far as his mouth.

The unyielding set to his lips didn't slacken a bit. "Do you feel better now?"

"Much better." She glanced toward the kitchen door and back at him. The sound of the children's voices drifted close. "We need to talk where we can't be disturbed."

He didn't question her need for privacy. "Let's go into my office."

He cupped his palm under her elbow and ushered her through the sparsely decorated house. She barely had time to appreciate the high-vaulted, cedar-lined ceilings and the cozy fireplace at the end of the living room before he led her into a smaller room at the other end of the house.

Three pieces of furniture were the only accessories. Papers were strewn haphazardly across what she assumed to be a large desk. A neutral-tone file cabinet stood against the back wall, while an easy chair covered with blue velvet sat off to the side.

Devlin shut the door behind them. As he turned toward her, she saw the tense lines fanning from the corners of his eyes.

"You're sick, aren't you? What is it? Cancer? Some kind of blood or liver disease?"

"No, I'm not sick." Whether she was ready for it or

not, the moment of truth had arrived. Bracing herself, she lifted her chin. "I'm pregnant."

At first, Abby's words didn't register in Dev's mind. He'd been preparing for the worst. Now all he could do was stare at his wife, whose curvy figure was clearly defined in fitted jeans and an ivory-colored sweater. Her face, smoothly textured and still a bit pale, looked composed. Although she hadn't gained any weight, he noticed her hands rested protectively over her stomach.

"Pregnant?" The word tasted metallic and unfamiliar.

"The doctor figures the baby will be born in early September," she said quietly.

"I see," he said, even though his mind wasn't quite functioning at full power.

She managed to raise a half smile. "I didn't think there was any danger of my getting pregnant. John and I were never able to have another child, so I just assumed..." Her voice trailed away. She dropped into the soft cushions of the blue velvet chair. Her gaze shied away from his as she looked down at her fingers, which were digging into the padded armrest. "I know this isn't something either of us planned or discussed, and I will take full responsibility for this baby."

Dev didn't know which reality surprised him more—her pregnancy or her calm acceptance of her condition.

His ex-wife hadn't taken either of her pregnancies well. Pregnant when they married, Linda alternated between resentment for losing her shape and whining that he wasn't showing her enough attention.

The fact that Abby wasn't railing at him, accusing him of deliberately foisting a child on her, reassured him somewhat. Abby wasn't a flag-waving career woman like Linda.

That's why he'd married her. His new wife put family first.

Abby had been juggling two stay-at-home jobs when they'd met, so she could raise Paige instead of sending her to day care. He wanted that kind of mother for his sons.

He was heartily thankful Abby wasn't like his first wife in either temperament or looks. That's what had drawn him to her in the first place. Abby wasn't one of those breath-stopping beautiful, look-but-don't-touch-type women like Linda. He classified Abby as a hands-on-type woman.

He hadn't wanted a woman as badly as he wanted Abby since he was teenager. His red-hot desire for her had caught him off guard, knocking aside his barriers. He certainly hadn't been able to keep his hands off her, and she'd seemed just as delighted in having them on her.

Hell, they'd struck enough sparks to create five kids. Her condition shouldn't have come as a surprise. Even if he had been using protection, it might not have withstood the onslaught of desire that had flared fiercely between them.

Even now he could remember the satiny smoothness of her skin. How rich and enticing her shoulder-length brown hair had looked spread across the pillow. How strokable and sensitive her lush curves were to a man's fingertips.

Just being in the same room with her made his palms itch to hold her, touch her and make her cling to him in passion.

Cool it, Hamilton. *You can't risk it. You've already violated the contract once.*

If he allowed lust to gain the upper hand, he'd destroy the life his sons needed. He couldn't allow that to happen again. They'd already lost one mother and were suffering for it. Jason didn't trust women. Riley was obsessed with them, always trying to get their attention. They needed a woman in their lives. Someone they could count on. Someone who would care for them more than a baby-sitter or housekeeper would.

They needed Abby.

Abby's straight-backed posture, which reminded him of a prisoner who awaited pronouncement of her sentence, made him realize that she was waiting for his response.

He searched for words that would at least reassure her he intended to keep his end of their deal from now on. "You didn't create this child alone. I'd say we both were contributors."

Color surged to her face. "I don't know what happened that night. It's never happened like that. I've never...I mean...it was never..." She stopped talking and looked away from him.

She nibbled on her lush lower lip—something he remembered doing himself not too long ago.

"Never?" He had no business being pleased by Abby's artless confession. Not when that passion had destroyed his common sense. Yet he was.

Abby turned toward him again with a lingering cautiousness. "You don't mind about the baby, do you?" she asked.

Her question stopped him short.

"Mind?" He masked any emotion from showing on his face. "Do you mind?"

Abby's hands curved over her still-flat belly, a determined protectiveness entering her eyes. "I want this baby very much. But not every man likes being surprised."

"Neither does every woman." The tension eased within him.

He should have seen that Abby probably hadn't been any more sure of his reaction to the news than he had been of hers.

It came as a bit of a shock to realize that Abby wasn't sure of him. Even Linda hadn't questioned or doubted his commitment to his family. He wanted Abby to understand that his devotion to this baby and to her would be as strong as it was to his sons. "This baby will be welcomed by both of us." There was no hesitation in his voice.

Abby's posture visibly slackened in relief. She flashed him a blinding smile and then surprised them both by launching into his arms and planting a kiss on his mouth.

He barely had time to absorb the delightful taste of her when she pulled back. "Oh, I'm so glad. You don't know how worried I was."

Then, just as quickly, she was gone, and he found himself clutching cold air. She slipped through the door of his office and returned seconds later, carrying her purse.

Emptying the contents onto his desk, she rifled impatiently through the items. Finally she pulled a folded piece of paper from the mess and handed it to him. "I know a baby wasn't part of our deal—"

"Deal?" His hand closed around the paper but he made no move to open it. He still hadn't shaken off the effects of the kiss.

She didn't seem to notice his slow-witted idiocy. "You paid off John's gambling debts when we got married, and I promised to pay you back after my house in Cincinnati sold. But since the real estate market is soft in Ohio right now, it could take a while before I can repay you the money. And this baby will be an added financial strain."

An age-old coldness rose within him, hard and impenetrable. "I make more than enough money to feed this family and a dozen more children."

"Money's not the point."

"Then what is?"

She set the paper carefully on the desk. "I know your construction business is profitable, and I am utterly grateful to you for paying off John's bills. But those debts are still my responsibility. I have to consider Paige and the baby."

"They're protected under our contract. Nothing's changed. Our agreement stands."

"So far, that agreement hasn't stood for anything," she reminded him, her tone quiet and nonjudgmental but firm.

There was no hiding from the truth for either of them.

He knew she was referring to the passion that had swept out of control and provoked this scene. "It won't happen again," he stated through clenched teeth. "I give you my word."

A glimmer of weariness touched her smile. "Neither of us knows what the future will bring."

"You don't believe me?"

The look she gave him was sympathetic, tinged with a sadder-but-wiser wisdom. "I discovered a long time ago that promises rarely stand the light of day."

"Only if one person changes the rules." Like his ex-wife had. At first Linda accepted their individual roles. She stayed home with the boys and he earned the money. But then she went to work and discovered the power and freedom that went with earning her own money.

Was that what Abby was trying to do?

He studied the shadows engraved under her blue eyes and saw the vulnerability.

It dawned on him she wasn't trying to provoke him

but merely stating facts as she understood them. "Your husband did a real number on you, didn't he?"

She interlocked her fingers as if she needed something to hang on to. "We've both been married before, and we know there are no guarantees a marriage will last forever. All I'm asking is that we add an addendum to the original contract that protects everyone's interests."

"In what way?"

She gestured at the folded paper he held. "If you'd read the addendum—"

"You tell me what it says."

At his noncommittal tone, she squared her shoulders and lifted her stubborn chin. "Basically, it lays out the terms for repayment of the loan. I'll keep my own bank account so there won't be any confusion in case of a breakdown in the marriage. I've also listed the few assets that weren't sold to pay off debts. According to a divorce lawyer I spoke to, the rest of the new wording is pretty standard."

Disbelief gnawed through his gut. "You went to a divorce lawyer?" He struggled to hang on to his temper. Was she starting to feel hemmed in already? "You want out of the marriage?"

"No, of course not." Her surprised reaction seemed almost believable.

Almost.

Given how little he understood the female mind, he wasn't about to claim victory. Nor was he about to back down from finding out what in the hell was going on. "You think I'm going to kick you out or leave you destitute like your former husband did?"

"Did you think your first wife would put her career before your family?" she countered. "Did you believe she'd leave you with two boys to raise?"

"You're not Linda, and I'm not John."

"No, we're not." Her expression softened with a plea for understanding. "But I knew John several years before I married him. I thought I knew everything there was to know about him and then discovered I didn't know anything. Whereas, you and I have only known each other a few months. And during that time, we've been around each other only a handful of days. We really don't know what surprises the other has in store."

"This marriage will last."

"Will it?" She crossed the floor between them and laid a hand on the tight muscle of his arm. "We need to be practical. This is more than just you or me."

Dev wanted to reject her words, even though she made a heck of a lot of sense. He'd bought into the entire happily-ever-after package when he married the first time.

And he'd learned the hard price of being so gullible.

So had his sons.

Passion didn't last. It didn't put food on the table. It didn't provide a foundation for a family to rely on.

When he'd proposed to Abby, he'd decided it was best for all concerned to negotiate their union as he would any business deal. He'd used logic instead of romance.

He believed he'd succeeded until his uncontrollable lust had taken control.

He'd broken his word to Abby, and now she was pregnant.

Her unwillingness to trust him was understandable. He was getting what he deserved. They were both going to pay the price for his lapse.

He tossed the paper down on the desk and considered her rigid posture. She had a right to expect a few concessions—so long as they were reasonable. "You told me you didn't want to work outside the home."

"I don't." She sounded sincere, her clear blue gaze never wavering.

"Then what did you have in mind?"

"You told me you hated doing bookkeeping and were having trouble keeping up with your office work. I've got a good head for figures and could take over those duties. You can keep track of my hours and write them off against the debt."

He still didn't like it. Any of it. Yet, she was right about one thing. He did hate paperwork of any kind, and he'd rather have her work for him than for someone else. At the sight of her hopeful expression, he gave in. "All right, you can help me with the book work and payroll."

When her eyes started to beam with pleasure, he walked around the desk and stood in front of her, making sure their bodies didn't touch. "But I'm not signing the addendum. The original contract stands."

"But—"

He stopped her protest. "If we have too many papers between us, we'll be sure to mess up. I don't want to worry about making any more mistakes, do you?"

He wasn't about to screw up again. He intended to prove to Abby he was a man she could count on.

She frowned, eyeing him with uncertainty. "It's not going to be easy. For any of us."

"We'll make it work."

His flat statement didn't appear to reassure her. "Your Jason is going through those rough middle-school years. He's bound to resent having a stepmother, a stepsister and now a baby sibling, too. Riley and Paige will have to make major adjustments, as well. We're going to have to blend two families and make room for a fourth child." She took a shaky breath, a twinge of sadness pulling at the corners of her mouth before she continued, "We married before we had a chance to know each other. And now the lives of four other people will be affected by that decision. I don't want to fail four innocent children.''

"We won't let them down if we trust each other to follow the contract." He refused even to consider failure despite all the what-ifs. This marriage would be his first priority. He'd keep everything under control.

Abby resumed worrying her lip as she moved around the room, a frown disturbing the smooth texture of her skin. "There's something else you should know."

"What's that?"

"I'm not much of a cook. I've taken every cooking class imaginable, but somehow I never quite got the hang of it."

He kept his smile tucked inside. The tension lifted from his shoulders. "We'll get by."

She picked up a pen sitting on his desk and twirled it between her fingers. "I don't know what kind of toothpaste you use, or what you like to do on a typical Saturday night, or even what your favorite foods are."

He shrugged. "I use whatever brand is cheapest, I sometimes read a book or watch a movie on Saturday night and I'll eat whatever you put in front of me."

"How well do you like eggs?"

"Well enough." There was something oddly fascinating and endearing about having her worry about what to feed him.

"Eggs three times a day can be a bit boring."

He didn't bother to contain his amusement this time. "I'll take my chances."

She tilted her head and eyed him with skepticism. "You're a brave man."

"That's what I've been trying to tell you."

Chapter Two

Late the next morning, Abby awoke feeling more herself, the nausea having mercifully disappeared. A tender smile curved on her lips as she turned and looked at Paige and Princess, who were both sound asleep on the other side of Devlin's king-size bed.

The sixth snake had been discovered inside Riley's jacket pocket, but her daughter stoutly refused to sleep in her new bedroom with one snake still at large.

Sharing a bed with her daughter was not an uncommon occurrence. Since John's death, Paige often crawled in with Abby. She had a tendency to be a kicker, though, and it was a good thing Devlin had decided to camp out on the Hide-A-Bed. She doubted that his king-size bed would be nearly as comfortable with three people in it, plus Paige's feet.

Of course, this sleeping arrangement would only be temporary. Paige would eventually sleep in her own bed. Then Abby would have to contend with sleeping with

Devlin. And after what happened on their wedding night...

Steering her mind away from her new husband and the inexplicable havoc he seemed to wreak on her pulse rate, she looked around the room. The room had a romantic, woodsy scent and feel, due in part to the cedar-lined walls that were identical to those in the rest of the house. An antique dresser and mirror sat perched against the wall. The windows were covered with Venetian blinds and a beautiful landscape painting of peaceful waterfalls adorned the opposite wall.

Everything about the house and room reminded her of her six-foot-tall husband. Attractive. Solid. No fuss. The man and his home went together.

Turning on her side, she could see the rest of the room, including the big walk-in closet with neat rows of jeans lined up on shelves. There was a suit or two but no khaki pants or polo shirts.

Devlin was definitely the blue-jeans type. He favored comfort in his environment and his clothes.

She thought about her own clothes still packed inside the suitcases sitting at the foot of the bed and tried to imagine them hanging in the closet next to Devlin's. When her dresses and shirts filled in the empty spaces, she wondered if she'd start to feel more at home. More married. The reality of being here, sleeping in Devlin's bed and sharing his closet made this marriage seem more intimate than she'd imagined.

A niggling doubt crept into the back of her mind.

She'd learned years ago that the only person she could truly count on was herself. Accepting sole responsibility for herself had gotten her through many rough spots and insulated her from being too disappointed when her expectations of others failed.

She needed that insulation now more than ever.

Devlin had a power over her senses that stormed her defenses and made her forget to be careful.

When she'd met him two and half months ago at a party to celebrate his sister and her husband's fifteenth wedding anniversary, she had been in desperate straits.

The party had barely started when Abby got a call from Paige's baby-sitter to tell her the roof had started leaking again. Because Devlin was an independent contractor, he volunteered to go with her and check it out. He'd managed to temporarily patch the roof and then had returned the next day to make permanent repairs. The few hours he worked on the house had stretched into his spending the majority of the weekend with her. She'd protested the use of his vacation to work on her house. But he'd flashed her his toe-curling grin and said he'd nothing better to do.

Her daughter formed an instant attachment to Devlin, and surprisingly, he didn't seem to mind—not like Paige's own father, who never had an interest in childish games and abhorred jelly-coated fingers. Devlin took time to listen and talk to Paige. He even read stories to her. He became a hero in her daughter's eyes. And probably in her own, as well.

How could she resist a man who could nail down the roof and hunker down to a four-year-old's level to chat about imaginary playmates?

Abby hadn't been able to.

In the short space of that weekend, she discovered she and Devlin had a great deal in common. They'd both suffered major disappointments in marriage. Devlin's ex-wife had divorced him shortly after his youngest son was born and had moved to New York to further a high-powered career. Devlin had expressed his frustration about Jason's derogatory feelings toward women. He'd told her about Riley's being caught stealing another boy's school lunch, and his bewilderment over the counselor telling him Riley was trying to get Devlin's attention.

In turn, Abby had found it surprisingly easy to share the grim details of her husband's sudden death and the painful discovery of the huge debt he'd left behind. Once Abby started talking to Devlin, she couldn't stop. Facing the reality of selling their home and liquidating their assets, she'd told him about trying to get a loan, being turned down and searching for any options besides taking a job outside the home and putting Paige in day care.

Just being able to unburden herself to another adult had been a release in itself.

When the weekend was over and Devlin returned to Wisconsin, Abby had experienced an acute sense of loss.

Then two weeks later, Devlin showed up on her doorstep again, helped arrange for a baby-sitter and took her out to dinner. Later that night, he presented his proposition. He needed a wife and mother for his sons, and she needed financial stability in order to provide a good life for Paige.

With her options drying up, the bank threatening foreclosure and little money to make ends meet, Devlin's plan was an answer to Abby's prayers. The one thing she wanted to be was a mother. Raising Devlin's sons seemed logical and heaven-sent. Her only stipulation before agreeing to the marriage was that she would pay back John's debt.

She refused to be a financial burden.

Once she'd said yes, Devlin made arrangements for the speedy wedding. She didn't have time to second-guess her decision.

Everything went smoothly until after the wedding.

Paige's bout with chicken pox was complicated by an allergic reaction to the prescribed medicine. What should have been two weeks between the wedding and their move to Wisconsin stretched into six.

Because Devlin had been in the midst of a remodeling project, he could come to see them only once during that time. Even though they kept in touch by phone, the easiness that had existed between them prior to the I do's had disappeared.

The passion that had caught them unawares came at a cost. It destroyed their easy camaraderie. During the weeks that followed, lengthy uncomfortable pauses across the long-distance lines made her question the marriage and whether they'd done the right thing by marrying in haste.

What did they really know about each other?

She'd been here less than twenty-four hours and already they'd been buffeted by disenchanted children, closet space, jobs, snakes and the realization that a baby would arrive in their midst in less than seven months.

She placed her hand on her still-flat stomach. It was too late to reconsider. They had created a new life between them. Yet the future, stretching ahead of them, seemed blurry and uncertain at best.

They'd married for convenience, which had already been upstaged by a grand case of lust. What other potholes lay in their future?

Abby, my girl, you're getting ahead of yourself. At least she'd set down a few rules this time. She wasn't looking for love and neither was Devlin. That would make things a bit easier.

She'd been loved and abandoned so many times in her life, she knew better than to relax her guard and believe in rainbows and pots of gold. They were mirages she couldn't stake her future on.

Chewing on her lip, she stared up at the beams criss-crossing the ceiling and tried to review her options. The only thing she could do was to be a good mother to the children and work to pay off John's debts so Devlin wouldn't ever feel he had married a charity case.

No matter what, she'd never be that dependent or vulnerable again.

Abby eased her relaxed body out of the bed, padded across the braided rug covering the hardwood floor and stepped into the bathroom.

Twenty-minutes later, she was in the kitchen, checking the cupboards. She cautiously made friends with the big dog. He welcomed her with a wagging tail and a drooling tongue before jumping up and trying to lick her face. After tussling with him for a few minutes, trying to calm him down, she let him outside on a leash before rummaging through the refrigerator. Since it was almost eleven o'clock, the breakfast hour had come and gone. A good hearty lunch could go a long way toward building family togetherness.

Halfway through her preparations, a sleep-rumpled Devlin walked into the room, and her heartbeat zig-zagged. Bare-chested, wearing only a pair of well-worn jeans, he made her pulse rate pick up speed.

Settle down, Abby. You're a married woman with children in the house. You're not supposed to act like an obsessed teenager.

So why was she battling a crazy desire to fling herself into his arms and run her fingers through the thick curls of dark hair that trailed from the base of his throat and disappeared into the waistband of his shorts?

"What do you think you're doing?" An early-morning gruffness thickened his voice.

She tore her gaze away from him. "Fixing lunch. I stopped at an Italian take-out restaurant yesterday. This was supposed to be last night's dinner, but—"

"You should have woken me up, and I would have helped you."

She shook her head. "I heard you prowling around the house last night. You needed your sleep."

"I still do. Hulk snores."

She stopped what she was doing and tilted her head. "Hulk?" It took her a moment to realize he was talking about the dog.

"He insisted on sleeping with me."

She fought back a smile. "I'm sorry Paige kicked you out of your side of the bed."

He shrugged, a motion that put his well-developed muscles in motion. "I can wait. There's no hurry."

She was trying to ignore the rippling biceps and firm chest, when he suddenly moved closer and placed the back of his hand gently on her forehead.

"What?"

"How are you feeling this morning? Stomach still kind of queasy?"

She blushed at the reference to her ungraceful arrival yesterday. "I'm not sick." Sliding out from under his hand, she tried to put a safe distance between them. She had a hard time thinking straight when he touched her, even when it was impersonal. "I'm pregnant, and last night I was exhausted."

He didn't appear convinced. "You shouldn't have made that trip in one day."

His perusal had an unsettling effect on her nerves. She made a stab at redirecting the conversation. "If you'd like, there's time for you to take a shower while I get lunch ready.''

She leaned down and pulled a big bowl from the lower cupboard. Straightening, she saw Devlin's smoldering gaze eye her gaping, loose-fitting shirt. The sea green of his gaze darkened to the passionate richness of jade.

Warmth flooded through her body. She licked her dry lips. ''Lunch should be ready in about twenty minutes.''

His gaze zeroed in on her moist mouth. ''If you say so.'' He made no attempt to move away.

Jason's voice broke through the sensuous haze holding Abby hostage. ''You two going to lock lips, or are you going to let Hulk in before he rips down the back door?''

Abby jerked. She heard the hostility in Jason's voice at the same time as she noticed Hulk's howling at the back door. ''I'm sorry.'' Feeling awkward, she pushed her hair away from her face in a self-conscious motion. ''I forgot I let the dog out. He's probably hungry.''

She headed toward the door, but Devlin's arm stopped her.

He frowned at his son. ''Never mind. Jason can take care of the dog.''

Riley, wearing slippers that were too big for him and looking as if he'd just climbed out of bed, shuffled into the room. ''You guys were kissing? Why do I always miss the good stuff?''

''What do you know about the 'good stuff'?'' Jason said, smirking, his tone rich with thirteen-year-old superiority. ''You're just a kid.''

''I can't help that.'' Riley scowled. ''They don't let us have sex on the playground.''

Abby burst into laughter.

Devlin didn't appear as amused. ''Riley, go with your

brother and take care of Hulk. Then you two can get dressed.''

"Aw, Dad..."

"You, too, Jason."

Jason gave an I-don't-give-a-rip shrug and sauntered to the door. "Come on, brat. It's boring in here."

Abby watched them leave, her amusement dying away as fast as it had risen. "Jason didn't look too happy."

"It's cool to be cynical and grumpy at that age," Devlin said. "You get used to it after a while."

She nibbled on her lip, her forehead puckered with uncertainty. "Was he close to his mother?"

Shutters descended over Devlin's gaze. "Linda was close to her work. The rest of us were just in her way." Before she could question him further, he turned away. "I'm going to go take my shower and get dressed."

She watched him leave. The house seemed very cold all of a sudden.

While Abby added the final touches to their lunch, she heard sounds of bodies moving throughout the house. The murmur of voices could be heard occasionally.

Three times the kitchen door opened.

"My dad wants to know if you need any help," Jason said, his voice expressionless. He'd showered and changed into a plain white T-shirt and jeans.

"You could add another leaf to the table if you'd like," she suggested.

He let the door snap shut behind him.

Five minutes later, Riley stood in the same spot his brother had vacated. "Dad wants to know if you need some help." He'd tried to tame his hair with a comb but hadn't quite succeeded.

The tug on her heartstrings made it hard to resist the

urge to reach out and smooth the helter-skelter hair into place. "How about if you put the silverware on the table?"

He'd no sooner left the kitchen than Paige arrived towing a very tolerant Princess. "Mommy, me and Princess want to help, too."

"Princess and I," Abby corrected automatically. "After you put Princess back in the bedroom, wash your hands and you can put the napkins on the table, honey."

"Princess isn't dirty. She licks herself all the time. Can I just lick my hands clean, too?"

"No, you have to use real water and soap."

"But why?"

"Because you're not a cat." Abby turned her daughter around and gently pointed her toward the door. "Now, hurry up because we're going to eat pretty soon."

Paige heaved an exaggerated four-year-old sigh. "When I grow up, I'm going to be a cat."

"Okay, but today you're still a little girl with dirty hands. Scoot."

Ten minutes later, Abby had the plates ready. Carrying them into the dining room, she set plates in front of Paige and Riley while Devlin handed out his and Jason's. Then she carried her own small portion to the other end of the table. No one said anything as she seated herself directly across from Devlin.

The silence was almost deafening.

She gave Devlin a thumbs-up. "Well, shall we eat?"

He picked up his fork. "This looks delicious, doesn't it, boys?"

Riley grabbed his fork and eyed the circles of pasta Abby had artfully displayed on each plate. He wrinkled his nose in confusion. "I didn't know you could eat these things."

Jason glared at his plate with even more suspicion than usual. He prodded the circles with his fork but didn't try to cut them. "What are they?"

"Breast implants," Riley answered before Abby could respond. "I saw them on TV."

Jason began to snicker as his father reached over and pulled the fork from Riley's hands. "That's enough, young man. You will be polite, or you can leave the table. Now, apologize to Abby."

Riley's face whitened, making his freckles stand out noticeably. "I'm sorry," he mumbled, his chin almost scraping his chest.

Abby didn't want their first meal as a family to be ruined. "This is ravioli, but I guess it does look sort of strange, doesn't it?"

Devlin gave Riley and Jason a behave-yourself-or-else look. "The boys and I have only eaten it out of a can. Having home-cooked meals is going to be a welcome experience, isn't it?"

An uneasy feeling started in the pit of Abby's stomach. "It's not exactly home-cooked. I just reheated it in the microwave." As Riley continued to stare at it dubiously, she said, "Paige loves ravioli, isn't that right, honey?"

Her daughter shook her head and frowned. "Not this kind. It tastes icky. I like the kind at home."

"May I be excused?" Jason asked. He pushed back his chair.

"You haven't finished the food on your plate," his father said.

"It's okay if—" Abby started to say.

Jason ignored Abby and glared at his father. "I'm not hungry."

"Tough." A brick building looked more flexible than Devlin's jaw. "Abby went to a lot of work to fix this meal, and you'll eat it or stay in your room the rest of the day."

"That suits me just fine." Jason threw his napkin on top of a plate and stood up. "I didn't ask her to fix me anything. You don't really think she is going to stick around, do you?" His voice dripped with derision.

"Jason—"

Jason stalked from the room without a backward glance.

"Mommy?" There was a pleading note in Paige's voice. "Can we go home now?"

"This *is* our home." Abby tried to sound more confident than she felt. "You can go upstairs, unpack your suitcase and put your clothes in the drawers of your new bedroom."

Paige's lower lip jutted forward. "I don't like that bedroom. I want to stay with you."

Biting back a sigh, Abby decided she didn't have enough energy left for an argument. The meal was already a bust. "We can discuss this later. Why don't you see how Princess is doing in the bedroom?"

After Paige left the table, Riley put down his fork. "May I be excused, too?"

Abby nodded. Scraping back his chair, he stood up and came over to where she sat. "Could we have stroganoff tonight? I really like that."

The wistful yearning in those big luminous eyes made her want to hug him. She hated to disappoint him. "I might not be able to fix it tonight, but I'll see if I can later this week." When he beamed at her, she asked. "Do you like eggs?"

He scratched his head, sending the rest of his hair into disarray as he considered her question. "I like them scrambled."

"Good. Scrambled, it is." She decided not to mention that any egg dish she made came out scrambled. They'd figure it out soon enough.

After the boy left, Devlin's gaze met hers across the table. She couldn't quite tell whether he approved or disapproved. She broke the silence growing between them. "I'm afraid Riley's going to be disappointed with my limited repertoire of meals."

"I didn't marry you for your cooking skills." He paused. "Look, I'm sorry, Abby. They were deliberately rude to you. I'll have Jason apologize to you later."

She picked up Riley's plate, using a fork to empty the rest of his food onto hers. She'd lost her own appetite. "Don't say anything to him for now. We've got to give them time to adjust."

He shook his head. "I think it would be a good idea to hire a nanny. Someone to help you—"

"No. We agreed that I would take care of the children."

"For how long?"

Surprise kept Abby in her place. "What are you talking about?"

"You've already talked to a divorce lawyer once." His hands had curled into tight fists, cutting the blood from his knuckles and producing a stark whiteness to his skin. "How long before you decide this marriage isn't worth the effort and contact that divorce lawyer about drawing up a different kind of contract?"

Her mouth dried as she tried to compose her answer. "I'm not contacting a divorce lawyer. We'll need to give the kids time to adjust."

"And what if they don't?"

She recognized the scars his wife had left behind and wanted to erase the pain, but couldn't. Making promises she might not be able to keep would be the worst thing she could do. "I don't know. We'll have to take it a day at a time."

"For how long?"

She grappled for an answer and found the only one that she could give honestly. "I'm not a quitter, but I don't want the baby to be born into a family at war with each other."

Devlin dragged back his chair, the sound as grating to the nerves as a dentist's drill. The tense lines in his face masked whatever emotions swirled inside him. "I'll speak to Jason and have him apologize before dinner."

She flinched as the door to the house shut with a slam behind him. Utter fatigue swarmed through her, and she leaned back into her chair.

They weren't exactly starting out like the Brady Bunch.

Paige didn't like her new room. Jason believed she'd pack her bags and run at the first sign of trouble. Riley— bless his adorable freckled face—believed she'd raided the surgical ward at the hospital to prepare lunch. And her brand-new husband didn't trust her to stay for the long run.

How were they ever going to become a family? What kind of life would this be for her unborn child?

She squeezed back a tear that threatened to roll down her face.

What kind of life was this going to be for any of them?

Chapter Three

On a scale from one to ten, Devlin figured he'd just scored a minus seven. That might be on the high side. Patience had never been his long suit. He'd always chosen the most direct path to get what he wanted. But in this case, forcing the issue with Abby could have been a serious miscalculation. He refused to make the same mistakes he'd made with Linda. Abby deserved more from him.

She probably thought she'd married a dictator. He'd certainly behaved like one.

But before he went back inside, he needed to clear his head. He did his best thinking outdoors where he could physically work through his frustrations. Nothing uncluttered his mind better than swinging an ax or pounding a hammer.

Heading straight for the woodpile on the south side of the shed, he covered the ground with long powerful strides.

He didn't flinch as a frigid blast of February air took

a mean swipe at his exposed cheeks. The brutality of the weather and the starkness of the scenery fit his surly mood. The sky hung with overcast clouds, a blah backdrop to the carpet of snow covering every inch of landscape. It would be several months before spring would dare show its face. Winter still had a strong grip.

He crossed the ice-glazed driveway and crisp snowpacked ground. Grabbing a crudely hacked log, he placed it on the old stump. He picked up his favorite ax and swung it high over his head, bringing it down with all the force he could muster. The surge of energy released his pent-up emotion.

He'd bought this place after Linda left. The chic house he and his ex-wife had bought when they first moved to Humphrey had pleased Linda more than it ever suited him. He had always preferred to live in the wide-open spaces, where a man rose and went to bed with the sun.

When he was in college, he tried to adjust to city life as he attended the required courses for an architecture major. By the end of his third year, he'd had enough. He knew there was no way he could face working in glassy-towered buildings where fluorescent lights were the natural source of light. He needed more. He needed more freedom and more fresh air.

For him, living in this area of the country was as close to heaven as a man could get. He was a man who hungered for the physical connections with the environment and with those around him. That's why he'd chosen to become a contractor. He could be a part of Wisconsin's four seasons. He'd visited other areas of the country and found their insipid seasons draining. The challenge of Mother Nature's midwestern mood swings invigorated him. The merciless punch of winter could be as potent as a boxer's left hook. And the summers could wring dry one's sweat pores, but he never tired of the transitions.

Not the way he had tired of his marriage.

When it came to family life, he craved predictability and tranquillity.

Linda had stayed eight years. A lifetime of conflict, strain and tiptoeing around each other. When she'd left, he'd struggled to put his life back together again.

Building this house had helped him deal with his anger and rid him of his sense of failure. Each nail he sank into the wood represented a future for his sons. Here they could thrive without the hostility that had become a constant in the fabric of his marriage.

There had been several years after the divorce when life had been good for all of them. They were getting along. The boys were growing. They didn't have a fancy life, but they had each other. They had him.

However, during the past year, both boys had gone through some rough patches. Devlin had tried to deal with each of Riley's scrapes with an honest and forthright discussion. The school counselor had insisted Riley was acting out his need for more attention. But Devlin couldn't always be there when his kids needed him most. He had to work. And as a result, he couldn't fill that void in his sons' lives.

They needed a mother figure. A nurturer. Someone who would be there when they came home from school and who could bridge the empty spaces.

Still, Devlin resisted the idea of getting married again. He'd already failed at marriage once.

He didn't believe in love, an emotion that lasted about as long as one of those melodramatic soap-opera relationships. There was no way he'd get caught up in that kind of emotional roller coaster again, and yet that's what most of the women he met wanted. They expected things from him he couldn't provide.

What he had needed was a woman who could be a mother to his kids. Someone with staying power. Someone who wasn't looking to make a name for herself in the business world.

Meeting Abby at his sister's house had seemed like a gift from above. It didn't take long to pry all the pertinent information from Gayle about her attractive neighbor. It took him even less time to come to a decision.

Marrying Abby had seemed as logical as donning a comfortable pair of work boots. She was the perfect fit and met all his basic requirements. Most important, she liked kids. She didn't have any grandiose desire to be a superwoman, juggling a family with a job. He liked her old-fashioned family values and the fact that she wanted to stay home.

Yep, he'd found a woman of pure gold all right.

He had everything under control. Or so he thought.

As he took another whack with his ax, an image of Abby on their wedding night formed in his mind.

Perspiration slicked his palms and suddenly the ax flew from Devlin's hand and stabbed the ground.

Astounded, he glared at the tool.

You've got to keep your mind on what's important and your pants zipped from now on, Hamilton. It was no wonder Abby was trying to lay down new rules. You screwed up, big time.

He had to honor his word if he was going to make this marriage work.

He'd already had one woman leave his sons high and dry. But he also realized he'd have to trust Abby on certain matters with regard to his sons. That wouldn't be easy since he'd been the chief decision maker for the past five years.

Today's meal hadn't been a promising beginning for the future. Even a woman like Abby was bound to have her limits. She grew up as an only child. Would she eventually get tired of the novelty of living in a makeshift blended family? Jason certainly wasn't going to cut her any slack. As for Riley, he appeared to like Abby and she him. But who knew how long that could last?

He retrieved the ax and swung at the log again, this time making a solid hit and causing the wood to splinter straight down the middle. No sense trying to second-guess the future.

He needed to go back inside and face Abby. She was probably regretting she'd ever asked him to fix her roof, let alone married him. He certainly wouldn't blame her.

Picking up the two halves of the log, he tossed them into the wheelbarrow sitting nearby. Then, taking the hatchet, he buried the point into the stump.

He knew what he had to do. The mistakes of his past would not be the lot of his future, not if he could help it. Making a bad habit was all too easy. Breaking it later would be next to impossible. He'd just have to keep on top of things as best he could and make sure Abby didn't get overwhelmed with the kids, the house and whatnot. He didn't expect everything to be a snap, but he figured with a little common sense and patience he could make everyone happy.

Turning around, he started toward the house.

His decision to trust Abby and use a little patience zapped from his brain when he arrived in the kitchen and spotted his wife perched on a shaky ladder. Abby, seeming oblivious to the danger, was reaching into a far corner of the top cupboard. As the ladder started to teeter, a fist of fear knocked the air from Devlin's lungs.

Acting on sheer reflex, he rushed forward and swung Abby off the wooden slats.

The suddenness of his movements caused the ladder to flounder and Abby to gasp, "Devlin?"

They both jumped as the ladder crashed to the floor.

Devlin didn't release her immediately, absorbing the heat and scent of her as he fought to regain mastery over his breathing. It didn't help, either, that her cushy derriere was cradled just inches above a vital area of his body.

Glaring at her, he growled. "What in the hell are you doing?" His heart was beating faster than a stampede of wild steers. How was he supposed to acquire patience when she risked her neck on a ladder?

Abby wiggled out of his arms. "I was rearranging a few things." Hooking a wayward curl behind her ear, she eyed him with uncertainty. "But if you object…?"

The rippling tension slowly slid off his shoulders. Raking his fingers through his hair, he shook his head. "I don't care if you want to put the spoons and forks in the bathroom closet, but let me know when you need to reach something above your head. I don't want you falling and hurting yourself…or the baby."

She gazed at him through the feathered arches of her long eyelashes. "Do you want me to carry a box of bandages with me, too?"

Her wry tone penetrated his thick skull. A sheepish redness eased up his neck. Reaching down, he picked up the ladder. "Did I sound like a card-carrying member of the Idiots-R-Us Club?"

"I think we're both a bit tense."

"Yeah, that's one way of putting it." If only she knew. He'd been tense ever since she'd walked into the house, but it didn't have a thing to do with that tipsy ladder or her wanting to change a few things. "What did you want to move?"

She pointed to a large blue bowl on the top shelf. "That might be good for stirring up eggs."

He lifted the dish and set it on the counter. "What else?"

"I'll take care of the rest."

"It might be better—"

"No, it wouldn't," she said, a hint of steel lurking ominously in the back of her eyes. "I need to learn my way around the kitchen and the easiest way for me to do that is to start doing things."

She crossed her arms in a pose that said she was standing her ground.

A glow of heat built in his loins and fanned upward as her gutsy stance drew attention to the nice thrust of her bosom. In contrast to the grim chill outside, the kitchen hummed with a scintillating warmth that didn't have anything to do with the physical room temperature, but with the sweetly mussed woman in front of him.

There was nothing overtly sexy about Abby or the casual clothes she wore. Yet, the package she presented— soft, curvy, with blue jeans that hugged the enticing curve of her hips and a soft sweater that cherished the distinctive swell of her breasts made him think of nothing else but sex.

He was suddenly hot. Too hot for the coat he wore. Too hot for his own skin. He understood the Scandinavian custom of rolling in the snow after sitting in a spa. That's the only thing that stood a chance against the steam permeating him.

As he started to pull off his jacket, Abby picked up a small notebook lying on the counter. "If it's okay with you, I'll need to go into town and pick up a few groceries."

He shrugged his coat back on. "I'll drive you. Jason can watch the kids."

She tucked back the curl that had sprung loose again. "You don't have to do that. I'm used to shopping on my own and finding my way around strange places."

Her statement drew his attention away from his physical urges as he wondered how many times in the past she'd had to deal with strange places and strange people. "I need to have you cosign the bank account. Now is as good a time as any."

"I'm keeping my own bank account, remember?"

Patience, Hamilton. Devlin tamped down his frustration. "But you'll be paying for the groceries out of our joint account." When she hesitated, he reminded her, "That's part of the terms we laid down in the contract."

"I suppose you're right." She traced a finger around the edge of the notebook, flicking the corners nervously. "Money is always an awkward thing to discuss, isn't it?"

He casually reached into his pocket and pulled out the car keys. "Not if we don't make it one."

She didn't respond to his suggestion. Instead she snapped the notebook shut and put it in her canvas purse. "I'll be ready to go into town in five minutes. Would that be convenient for you?"

Devlin recognized avoidance when he heard it. Abby hadn't argued with him, but she hadn't agreed, either. In other words, she still meant to keep her own bank account. There was nothing more he could say at this point without setting her back up further than it was. So long as she agreed to share the account that would cover all their personal needs, she met the letter of their agreement. That didn't mean he had to like it.

That didn't mean he wouldn't do everything in his power to change her mind, either.

As Devlin steered the late-model family-size car onto the paved county road and drove them toward town, Abby wished she could banish her spine-tingling uneasiness.

They'd been so comfortable with each other when they first met, laughing at the same silly stories Paige had created, enjoying the same uncomplicated movies.

Now all the simple friendship had fled, as if they were total strangers, facing each other for the first time. They were tiptoeing around each other, careful not to tread on each other's feelings, but not connecting, either. Beneath the prickly level, an awareness simmered, causing this nerve-tensing atmosphere. Would it have existed if they hadn't gone to bed together on their wedding night?

Did knowing each other in the biblical sense undermine everything they'd set out to achieve?

She wasn't sure what to do about the sizzling atmosphere. Or her undefinable feelings for Devlin.

Ignore them? Pretend they didn't exist and hope they would eventually disappear?

Devlin broke the silence between them. "Riley's looking for a home for his snakes. They'll probably end up in the science lab at school."

Abby relaxed a little bit. "Perhaps he could keep one."

Devlin shot her a quick glance. "Three kids, a baby, a dog and a cat in the house are enough wildlife to contend with, don't you think?"

"Will he be terribly disappointed?"

"For now, he is. By tomorrow, Riley will be trying

something else. Take it from me, he hasn't had a chance to bond with his slithery friends yet.''

She couldn't contain the smile. "I believe you."

"You should do that more often."

Startled, she met his jade gaze. "Do what?"

"Smile."

She tugged the edges of her coat together and interlocked her gloved fingers. "I guess I've been a little stressed."

"It's understandable. We probably both have."

She recognized this was his attempt to apologize. Her smile came easier this time. "It's understandable," she echoed his words.

He chuckled, the sound wrapping around her, filling her body with an intoxicating warmth that was instantly habit-forming.

Abby tried to keep her attention focused on the conversation instead of on watching Devlin's capable hands easily commandeer the car, anticipating each curve and bend in the road. His blunt-edged fingers were tanned and well-shaped, and in the swelling intimacy of the car, she recalled how they'd stroked her heated skin on their wedding night.

On some level, every part of her being responded to Devlin, the man. She had to be careful to keep a distance between them or she'd do something as stupid as...

She deliberately turned off that channel of stupidity.

Devlin's fist tightened around the steering wheel. "I guess neither one of us could have predicted what happened," he mused.

She shook her head. "Marriage and kids do that, don't they? We never quite know what we're taking on. What would you have done differently if you could do your first marriage over again?"

Devlin slowed the car as a tractor and wagon loomed ahead. "That's a question that haunted me for a long time after Linda left. I don't think either of us knew what the other one wanted in a marriage. By the end of it, we didn't care."

"What did you want?"

He frowned at the tractor ahead of him. "I wanted the small-town life where folks stop to talk to one another on the street corner or lend a helping hand when someone needs it. Those things were a part of my life when I was growing up, and I wanted them for my kids."

Abby didn't interrupt the silence that followed.

He flexed his fingers. "But Linda didn't like any of it. She hated the slow pace. She claimed Humphrey's local market didn't have the right kind of food, even though we usually ate just plain food. I liked being at home nights. She wanted to go to the theater or attend late-night committee meetings. I didn't mind that the post office closed for lunch or the township clerk only worked during the mornings. Linda thought it was archaic. We were like two shoes that didn't match. Maybe if I'd have compromised and agreed to move to Madison, we could have made it work."

She understood the derision in his expression. "But then you would have been miserable."

She couldn't see Devlin surviving well in a big-city setting. Although he'd looked fantastic in his suit the day they got married, she knew the clothes he wore now were a better fit for the man he was. One only had to look into Devlin's bold green eyes to realize he was who he was. Real. As real and as honest as the calluses on his hands.

That's what had appealed to her.

She was beginning to understand that was part of his danger, as well. It would be too easy to relax her guard and forget all the past had taught her. He was a man a woman could lean on. If she dared to lean.

Civilization greeted them as they reached the city limits.

"Does Humphrey have a preschool for four-year-olds?" she asked.

He nodded. "I spoke to the head teacher last week. They have an opening. She's expecting you to call sometime this week and bring in Paige for a visit."

His thoughtfulness on behalf of Paige caused a warmth to spread through her. "I appreciate your thinking of Paige and setting that up," she finally managed to say.

"That's what fathers and husbands do. They take care of details for their families."

Abby bit her lip. "Not all of them do."

He produced a rude sound. "They would if they were raised by my mother."

Abby smiled. She could picture Devlin's mother who always had a kind word for everyone. "I like your parents."

"The feeling is mutual."

Abby looked down at her gloved hands. "Did you tell them about the baby?"

"No."

She turned to stare unseeingly at the passing scenery. "I suppose they'll be rather shocked. After all—"

His chuckle brought her words to a stop. "My mother will be tickled pink and my father will probably buy me a case of cigars. I didn't tell them because my mother would have wanted to rush over here and fuss over you. I didn't think you were ready for that. She's delighted to see me married and can't wait to start fussing over you and Paige. Add a baby, and she'll want to move right in."

"That's sweet of her."

He snorted. "Wait until she wants to help you decorate the nursery. Or interrogates you about suitable names for the baby."

She wasn't sure if he was jesting or not. She'd met Devlin's folks on more than one occasion when they'd come to visit Gayle. When Abby had spoken to them on the phone after Devlin told them they were getting married, his father had decided to build them a china hutch for a wedding present and his mother had promised unlimited baby-sitting anytime they needed it. They were nice people.

"There are names your mother doesn't like?"

Devlin met her gaze through the rearview mirror. "I hope you aren't fond of the names Ralph or Ralphina."

"I think I can give them a pass."

"Good. There was a Ralph Hamilton who robbed the First National Bank thirty years ago, and we don't want to hang our child with that kind of reputation to live down."

"I wouldn't dream of it," she said, enjoying the spirit of the conversation. "And what about Ralphina?"

There was a distinct twinkle in his eye. "Name association, too similar to Ralph. Besides, my mother, who was a former schoolteacher, would point out that there are too many letters for a kid to learn to spell."

Abby decided she liked her new mother-in-law just that much more because she thought about children first. "Your mother is a smart lady."

"That's what she keeps telling my dad."

"How many years have they been married?"

"Almost thirty-five."

She shook her head in amazement. "They're very lucky, aren't they?" she said softly, almost to herself.

Devlin heard her. "According to my dad, each of us makes our own luck."

Is that why he had proposed to her? Abby wondered as Devlin found an empty stall in front of the Humphrey Market and angle-parked the car. By putting everything between them down on paper, was he making his own luck this time?

Yet his parents had made their marriage work. Anyone who had been around them could see the love between them. All thirty-five years' worth.

Even with their agreement, Abby couldn't help wondering if she and Devlin wouldn't need more than luck to guarantee their future. They had a lot of odds to overcome.

Abby knew Devlin tried to make the meeting at the bank easy for her. She shook the hand of Mr. Barrens, the banker, answered the appropriate questions and signed the suitable forms without voicing any objections. When she asked about opening a separate account, he'd made the transaction relatively painless.

Despite the resistance she sensed from Devlin, she did what she had to do. There was no way Devlin could understand what it was like to be so dependent, and there was no way to explain it.

When she'd married John, for the first time in her life she'd believed she could count on another individual. She'd trusted him, and in the process, nearly lost everything. It had been a cruel shock to discover after his death, he had wiped out their entire savings account and had placed a second mortgage on their house.

The creditors were demanding payment and she barely had enough money to keep Paige in shoes. Devlin's proposal had come just in the nick of time. Yet, the idea of being totally dependent on another man, even one of Devlin's character, wasn't wise.

It would be so easy to forget the mistakes she'd made and lower her guard. Devlin's home, his sons and the promise of a future were something she'd always wanted. Yearned for from the bottom of her heart. But she had Paige to think about. And now the baby. She couldn't risk them, or Riley and Jason, either. Children were so vulnerable. If this marriage didn't work out...if Devlin and she let each other down...

She had to be prepared no matter how cushy and secure-looking the view was from the inside of this family situation. Nothing lasted forever. Nothing. Expectations ultimately led to disappointment.

After they left the bank, Devlin directed her to the local market.

She had just pulled out her grocery list, as Devlin snagged a cart, when a voice said, "Devlin Hamilton, what is this I hear about you getting married and not even telling your oldest and dearest friends?"

Devlin winked at Abby before responding to a short, brown-eyed woman coming toward them. "I didn't tell you because then you'd tell that no-good husband of yours. I couldn't risk having him try to talk Abby out of marrying me before she was officially Mrs. Hamilton."

"I heard that," a deeper voice said. "Afraid I'd tell her about all your vices?" A tall man, whose head almost touched the fluorescent lights that hung from the ceiling, came around the corner of the aisle.

"You're my one and only vice and I've been trying to ditch you for years but you keep hanging around." Devlin's growl belied the wide grin taking center stage on his face.

From her husband's relaxed demeanor, Abby realized

immediately that this man and his wife were good and special friends of his.

"Abby, I want you to meet Rebecca and Cash Castner," Devlin wrapped his arms around Rebecca's shoulders and gave them a squeeze. "Becky is a good woman except for her bad taste in men."

"You're just jealous because I reeled in the only good woman in Humphrey." Cash's glib retort didn't contain an ounce of anger. Obviously the two of them had plenty of practice trading barbs.

"Hush, you two." Rebecca's rebuke accompanied a sprinkle of good-natured laughter. "You'll make Abby think we're uncivilized."

"Hey, this is Wisconsin. She's got to learn the truth sooner or later." Her husband didn't sound in the least bit repentant.

"Yep." Devlin agreed. "Truth is, Cash is something of a hillbilly by Wisconsin standards."

"What standards? This is the land of the cheeseheads." Cash grinned.

Rebecca frowned at her husband and then turned to Abby. "Ignore these two. They talk mean but they really are just two big hound dogs. Stroke them a few times and you'll have both of them feeding out of your hand."

"I'll keep that in mind." Abby sensed that Rebecca Castner knew how to keep her large husband in line. What was also evident was the deep love the other couple shared.

"Where are you from, Abby?" Cash asked.

"The Cincinnati area."

A coolness entered Cash's expression as his gaze slid from hers to meet Devlin's. "Another city girl, old buddy?"

Before Devlin could comment, Rebecca poked her

husband in the arm. "Behave yourself. You can't compare Linda and Abby. Linda grew up here and always wanted to leave. Abby's coming here to stay." She gave Abby an apologetic glance. "Don't pay any attention to this big lug. He's just worried that you won't have any interest in hearing about his and Devlin's old glory days on Humphrey's golden football field. Don't get him started on Humphrey's Yellow Falcons."

"There's nothing wrong with the Yellow Falcons. Abby should know something about the natives if she's going to live here."

Rebecca rolled her eyes. "Then we'll tell her about the year Devlin and I were elected to attend Boys and Girls State. And we'll also tell her about the first-class show choir we were all members of."

Cash grimaced. "She doesn't want to hear about that stuff."

"She doesn't want to watch you practice your Tarzan imitation, either."

The friendship and sense of history they all shared made Abby aware of how much of an outsider she was.

This wasn't the first time she'd faced this kind of suspicion. Outsiders always were suspect. She smiled at Cash and Rebecca. "I'll look forward to hearing about your glory days on the football field, Cash, if you can stand to listen to my stories about our all-state girls' basketball team."

A glimmer of respect flickered into Cash's face. Behind his chest-beating bravado, she saw glimpses of a smart man and a good friend. She knew then she would like both of the Castners and looked forward to getting to know them.

Devlin's warm palm slipped under Abby's elbow, establishing a supportive connection between them. "I didn't marry Abby so you could bore her with your obsession with pigskins, unless you want me to tell her about the time you got tripped by a cheerleader from the other team and ended up in the hospital with a concussion.''

Cash didn't miss Devlin's protective movement. The chill eased from his expression and he looked thoughtful. ''I'll give you the true story, Abby, since your husband doesn't have as good a memory as I do.''

Rebecca poked her husband in the ribs and gave him a sharp-eyed glare. ''Why don't you two go check out the cereals while I show Abby the fresh produce?''

Devlin didn't seem anxious to release her arm until Abby gently pulled it from his grasp. At his searching gaze, she offered him a smile before walking alongside Rebecca to the end of the aisle. ''Congratulations on your marriage. We're thrilled for Devlin.''

''Thank you.''

''You have a daughter?'' Rebecca asked.

Abby nodded. ''Paige is four years old.''

The other woman beamed. ''That's wonderful. Our daughter is the same age. Kelly will be tickled. Perhaps Paige could come over and play one day soon?''

''I'm sure Paige would like that. She misses her old friends.''

Rebecca nodded. ''Nothing means more to kids than their friends. At least your Paige is young enough to adapt.''

''I hope so.''

Rebecca's friendly manner made it easy for Abby to let down her guard. She had a feeling that Rebecca Castner was born smiling. ''Do you have any other children?'' Abby asked.

''Not yet. But I'd love to have an adorable son like

Riley someday." There was a hint of longing in Rebecca's voice before she banished it. "How are you getting along with Jason?"

Abby saw no reason to hide the truth. "The jury is still out."

"He'll come around." The smaller woman sighed. "He's a bit protective and he's been hurt more than he lets on."

Then Rebecca surprised her by reaching over and patting her arm, her brown eyes turning serious. "I'm sure this marriage is a big step for both you and Devlin. But frankly, I'm delighted for him. I was afraid Linda had soured him on marriage altogether. He's a good man who could use a little tender loving care."

"Yes, he is." Abby couldn't say any more than that. She doubted Rebecca would understand the contract she and Devlin had signed.

Their carts came to a stop next to the refrigerated-vegetables case. Rebecca reached for a package of carrots. "I have good instincts about people, and I know it's not going to be easy for you to blend two families. I hope you know, you've got a friend if you need one." She offered Abby the bag of produce and said in a low conspiratorial voice, "Riley loves carrots."

Abby took the bag from her. A lump of emotion rose in the back of her throat. "Thank you," she said.

Fortunately, any more confidences were halted as Devlin and Cash returned with armfuls of boxes.

Devlin placed several boxes in the cart. "I didn't know what you liked so I got an assortment of cereal."

"That's fine." She didn't care what she ate at this point.

As Cash began to unload his armful into his wife's

basket, Rebecca stopped his arm. "I don't want Kelly eating that sweet stuff."

"Good." Cash dropped the boxes into the cart. "These aren't for Kelly. They're for me."

Rebecca tsked. "You've got too much of a sweet tooth."

"That's why I married you, sugar." Cash grinned. "By the way, they've got fresh brownies in the bakery."

"Oh," she wailed. "Why did you have to tell me that?"

"There's a pan with your name on it."

"Lead the way, you sinful man."

They'd just turned the corner, when Rebecca popped around. "Why don't you two come over sometime soon and we can play cards or something?"

Devlin glanced at Abby.

She nodded. "It sounds like fun."

"Great." Rebecca waved and then disappeared out of view.

"How are you holding up?" Devlin asked. "You want to check out those brownies?"

Abby shook her head. "Chocolate isn't one of my weaknesses."

He lifted an eyebrow. "What is?"

Men with jade green eyes, was the first answer that came to mind. But she managed to keep the words from slipping off her tongue. Instead, she lifted the package of marshmallows and showed him her guilty secret.

He picked up the box of cinnamon candy. "Hot Tamales?"

She nodded soberly. "They're an addiction."

"That serious?"

"Very. I count every one that's in the box and know

if anyone else has been messing around with my Hot Tamales.''

He put them back into the cart and then leaned close to her. ''I'll be upset if anyone starts messing around with your Hot Tamales, too.''

Chapter Four

The trip home from town passed in silence.

Abby was suddenly exhausted and felt relieved to lean her head back against the headrest and close her eyes.

After they arrived home, Devlin deposited the grocery bags on the kitchen counter before retreating to his workshop.

Abby had just started unpacking the sacks when Riley barreled into the room. He dragged up a stool. "What did you get?"

She handed him a package. "Your dad said you liked chocolate cookies with marshmallow centers."

A big grin cracked across his face. "Cool. Can I have one now?"

"One or two shouldn't hurt your dinner appetite." She couldn't help smiling as she watched him rip open the bag.

She'd always wondered what it would be like to have a boy, but her imaginings hadn't quite measured up to the flesh-and-blood Riley. His carrottop hair looked as if his fingers had performed the hokeypokey through it. He wore a rumpled T-shirt that was several sizes too big, and his jeans proudly sported a ragged hole in each knee. His athletic shoes were caked with a thick layer of dirt, as if they had trounced through every mud hole between here and Timbuktu.

Paige lugged her ever-tolerant cat into the room. Spotting the groceries, she promptly dropped the cat and hoisted herself onto a chair next to Riley's. "Mommy, what did you get me? Did you get me my favorite cereal?"

"It's in the big bag." Abby frowned as she eyed her daughter's face. Colorful slashes adorned Paige's face. Rosy Sunset, if she wasn't mistaken. "Have you gotten into my makeup again, sweetheart?"

Her daughter pursed her smeared lips. "I only used a little, Mommy. Princess didn't like it much. She started to hiss and it kind of got all over the floor and stuff."

Abby wondered what other things in the house were wearing that shade of lipstick. She decided to hold off on the lecture until she could assess the damage.

Jason meandered into the kitchen. He didn't paw through the grocery bags like the two younger children. However, Abby saw his gaze scan the counter, inventorying all the contents.

She pointed to the sack on the left. "Your father mentioned you like peanut butter cookies. I picked up a couple of boxes."

Jason's top lip arced into a disinterested sneer. "I don't like store-bought cookies." Then he reached over and caught Riley's hand before his brother could grab another cookie. "You know Dad doesn't like you filling up on junk."

Riley tugged his arm free. "Jase, you should make

some of those sugar cookies again. I liked those the best.''

Abby looked at her oldest stepson. ''You bake?'' She kept her query low-pitched as if his answer didn't matter to her.

Jason's face flushed a bit. ''Somebody had to.''

''He's the best.'' Riley didn't seem perturbed by his brother's hostile expression. ''Grandma says he should become a chef. He can cook lots of stuff.''

Abby considered Jason's face. She recognized the tension exuding from his body. His defiance practically shouted at her. But she stored away the knowledge Riley had innocently offered.

''Hey.'' Riley lifted a carton from the last bag. ''Why are there so many eggs?''

''Don't you like eggs?'' she asked.

''They're okay.''

''Me and Mommy like them a lot,'' Paige said with serious four-year-old authority.

Jason finally sauntered over to the counter. He lifted a can and read the label. ''Dad can't eat this because he's allergic to mushrooms.''

''That's okay.'' Abby shrugged. ''We'll donate it to the Food Pantry. Aren't you supposed to take some canned goods to school?''

He shrugged and set the can down again. ''Those people might be allergic to mushrooms, too.'' He didn't look at her again as he left the kitchen. But she noticed he took a package of peanut butter cookies with him.

Devlin was a starving man.

Not physically starving. He'd had dinner with Abby and the kids, sharing another one of Abby's infamous scrambled-egg meals.

Over the past three weeks, he'd tasted combinations of scrambled eggs that would make a French chef take to his bed. Tonight's special had been a plateful of scrambled eggs smothered with canned chili. The night before, she'd served eggs with salsa. And the night before that had been eggs with ketchup.

It wasn't the egg dishes that were causing his hunger pangs.

He had no complaint against Abby's meals. They stuck to a man's bones and he figured he couldn't ask for more than that.

No, it wasn't lack of physical nourishment that made him seek out the solitariness of the barn on a cold late-winter evening with frustration eating a hole in his gut.

Heaving the trusty ax high, he glared at the log lying placidly in front of him and swung with all his might. The damn thing reminded him of the stupid contract that hung like a ball and chain from his neck. Unmovable. Flawed. And just there.

Except for their wedding night, he and Abby had done everything right to the letter of their agreement. He'd kept up his financial end of the bargain by finishing the Cramden job ahead of schedule and earning a hefty bonus in the process. Then he'd won the bid on two more construction jobs that would start as soon as the ground thawed.

Abby had abided by her written word, as well.

She kept the house neat, made sure the television stayed off until all the homework was finished and helped Riley if he needed it. Devlin noticed that his youngest son, who was as smart as a whip, had suddenly required a great deal of assistance over the past three weeks. The little devil was greedily lapping up having Abby at his beck and call.

Paige, on the other hand, still hadn't moved into her own bedroom, insisting her cat didn't like the new room. However, Devlin had noticed she occasionally went into the room to check on things.

Jason stayed in his room most of the time when he was in the house. He ventured out only when it was time to go to school, when it was time to eat or when he needed something. Other than that, he kept a respectable distance from the others. His oldest son didn't give his trust easily. Especially to a woman. There'd been problems in the past with some of his women teachers. But gradually he'd get used to them after a testing period.

He needed time and space. Fortunately, everyone seemed to respect that and gave him plenty of both.

Overall, as a family, they were getting by.

If only Devlin could say the same for himself.

His increasing desire for Abby was getting out of hand, and that's what drove him outside every night.

He was a physical man, and all this careful politeness was grating on his nerves. The gnawing ache in his loins stemmed from an overwhelming desire to make love to his wife. The abstinence was unnatural.

If he stayed in the house, he was afraid he was going to break the understanding he had with Abby and do something they'd both regret.

He'd always been honest in his business dealings. He'd promised Abby this marriage would be platonic. Signed a piece of paper stating his intentions. The fact that he'd broken his word once was one transgression too many. He was lucky she'd decided to stay with him and see this marriage through.

He was fortunate she wasn't holding this pregnancy against him, but Abby, luckily for him, wouldn't think of doing such a thing. She loved kids. Heck, she even put up with Jason's moodiness. Devlin figured it was only a matter of time before she got past the wall his oldest son had put up between them. She had a way about her that got under your skin and hooked you before you realized you'd been pricked.

That's what he was. Hooked and bleeding.

Who would have thought a pint-sized woman who couldn't cook anything but scrambled eggs could reel him in?

Every morning she pored over the countless cookbooks she'd brought with her from Ohio. She'd read through each recipe thoroughly, making copious notes. Then she'd head to the kitchen, rummage through cupboards and draw up lists before driving to the grocery store. An hour later, she'd return home with more eggs.

It was downright unbelievable the way she could devote hours at a time intensely studying a cookbook. And after all that time spent planning and studying, she'd end up with the same dish.

Eggs. Scrambled eggs.

It was the damnedest and sexiest thing he'd ever seen. And he wanted her more than he'd ever thought he'd want a woman.

Staring down at that pliant log in front of him, he thought about Abby and taking a slow drink from her tempting lush lips. That was just the first course. From there he'd feast on the silky smoothness of her breasts. Cup the curve of her nicely curved derriere. As for dessert...

Don't even think about it, Hamilton, he ordered himself. He had another long, cold night ahead of him on the lumpy Hide-A-Bed, tucked in between a dog that snored like a drunken sailor and a cat whose purr resembled a rusty faucet.

You'd better learn to live with it. He grunted. Yeah, right. By the year 2020, he should be used to it. By that time, he surely would be too old and tired to walk around in this state of semiarousal. Surely.

Posing the log just so, he lifted the hatchet high—

"Devlin?"

The voice caught him off guard. He fought to control the tool before he buried it into the side of his leg. When the ax did descend, it tore off a small chunk of the log before collapsing to the floor.

Abby appeared at his side, placing a hand on his elbow. "Oh, dear. Are you okay?"

"I'm fine." Try as he might, he couldn't make his tone sound natural. He still hadn't vanquished from his mind the image of Abby's naked body.

"What happened?"

He searched for an explanation and found a lame one. "My arm stiffened up."

"Does that happen often?"

Only every time I'm around you, he thought with self-loathing. To her he said, "I slept on my back last night. Everything has a tendency to get stiff."

That was the understatement of the year.

Her blue eyes peered into his, concern chiseling a path across her forehead. "That bed isn't big enough for you. Why don't I sleep with Paige in her bed—"

"No," he cut her off.

"No?"

He wished he didn't sound so desperate. "It's better if you keep the bigger bed. That baby is going to start kicking pretty soon and you'll need lots of support."

She didn't comment right away, chewing on the corner of her lip in contemplation. "Perhaps the three of us could fit in the bed. If you don't mind getting kicked by Paige's feet...."

"I'm fine."

She took her hand from his arm. "Well, if you're sure..."

He wasn't sure of anything except that it wouldn't be a good idea for them to share the same bed. At least not until the age of sixty-five, then he should have his lust under control. Sexual appetites diminished by retirement age. They had to.

She reached down and picked up the ax. Carefully handing it to him, she said, "I thought maybe we should have a talk."

Was it his imagination, or did she appear a bit paler than usual? "What's wrong? The baby?"

She gave him a reassuring smile. "The baby's fine and so am I."

"One of the kids? Has Jason been rude?"

"No, it has nothing to do with the kids." Her tone soothed even though her eyes were watching him closely. "Are you sure you're okay? You seem awfully tense. Do you want me to massage your shoulders?"

He restrained a groan at the mere thought of having her hands on him. He shouldn't risk it, yet he didn't have the strength to turn away when temptation took the upper hand. "Why don't we go into the house?"

She frowned. "I didn't intend to take you away from your work. I know you've been busy...." Her voice trailed away as she eyed the rows and rows of wood stacked along three sides of the shed. It didn't take an ace detective to determine he had cut enough wood for three hard winters and then some.

He didn't want her thinking too long and hard about

why he was so damn intent on becoming a world-class lumberjack.

He propelled her toward the door.

Once they were inside, he directed her to the office. It was the only place he could think of where they wouldn't be disturbed.

After he closed the door, Abby pointed to the chair. "If you sit there, I can reach your shoulders."

"You don't have to rub my shoulders."

"Yes, I do," she said quite firmly. "You've given up your bed and now you're paying the price. The least I can do is ease out the kinks. Besides, I like having something to do while I talk. It's more relaxing."

For her, maybe. How was he supposed to keep his mind on her words when her hands were putting his body through an exquisite torture?

He gritted his teeth and decided this was his penance for letting his desires and fantasies take control. He'd probably endure less agony if he donated his body to science while he was still alive.

"It's not surprising you couldn't cut that log," she mused. "The knots in your back are as large as Mount Rushmore. One of my foster mothers told me that you should always listen to your body."

He preferred to have *her* set up intimate communication with his body but knew that wasn't an option for either of them. "How many foster mothers did you have?"

"Twelve."

His gaze narrowed. "Why so many?"

"Situations change. Sometimes, they had too many kids. One family decided to leave the foster-care system and adopt a set of twins. Another moved to a different state when the husband got a better job. Sometimes peo-

ple discovered they weren't cut out to deal with more
kids than their own." She paused. "I have to admit, as
a teenager I didn't make it easy."

He could hear in her voice the secret pain she tried to
hide. "That must have been tough."

Her rubbing motion slowed for a bit before resuming
stimulation of his flesh. "It's not so bad if you don't
count on anything. You learn to keep loose and be flexible."

"And keep your suitcase packed?"

She laughed but Devlin heard the strain behind the
sound. "Sometimes it seemed that way."

Devlin's fingers curled into a tight fist. He wanted to
punch somebody. But what did he punch? The system?
Her parents who had died? The foster families whose
good intentions couldn't understand a teenager's growing
pains?

A new ache unfolded within Devlin. He wanted to take
Abby in his arms and banish all the loneliness.

But his commitment to her tied his hands to his side.

That's what he'd promised her. If only he had realized
how much more she needed before he'd proposed this
marriage. Somehow, providing a roof over her head
didn't quite make the grade. She deserved to be loved
and cherished. No one deserved happiness more than
Abby.

If only he'd realized how much they both needed and
wanted. But he didn't. Now they were caught in the net
created by his own shortsightedness. He couldn't blame
anyone but himself.

"Relax, you're tensing up again." She ran her hand
over his tight muscles. "It wasn't all bad, you know."

He didn't believe her for one moment but forced his
body to loosen.

She cleared her throat and changed the subject. "You haven't introduced me to your bookkeeping system yet."

"Bookkeeping system?"

"I want to start repaying that loan." Her voice was cool and impersonal, a sharp contrast to the sensual havoc she dealt his body. "The house in Ohio hasn't had any offers yet and I want to start repaying the loan."

He couldn't answer right away as she went to work on the ache in his shoulder blade, her fingers finding the sensitive cords of muscle. The last thing he wanted to discuss was money. Talking about anything seemed ir-reverent and irrelevant in the wake of the magic she evoked.

She stopped kneading his shoulder. "Devlin?"

"We can work on the books whenever you like." Hell, he'd sell his soul to the devil as long as she didn't stop. Having her touch him like this was almost worth the agony of sleeping with Hulk and Princess. Almost.

"Perhaps you could take me through the records to-morrow night after dinner."

"Fine."

He grunted. Words were too much effort.

A few minutes passed before she said, "I went to the doctor today."

That caught his attention. He turned his head. "Every-thing okay?"

"It was just a routine checkup. All he did was check my blood pressure and review my records that had been sent from Ohio."

"Your blood pressure was okay?"

"Yes."

"The doctor didn't think you were too thin?"

Her gaze glinted with amusement. She lowered her

arms to her sides and moved away from the chair. "Are you telling me I'm too skinny?"

"I didn't say that."

A rosy hue darkened her face but she didn't back down. "You prefer a plump wife?" she teased.

Within the intimacy of the four walls and with his body still humming from the sweet sensations of her touch, he couldn't resist the urge to reciprocate. He leaned back into the chair and interlocked his fingers behind his head as if pretending to give her question a great deal of thought. "I prefer a healthy woman who knows how to take care of herself and her family. A woman with eyes as blue as Lake Michigan, a shape that teases a man's appetite and a smile that raises his pulse."

She swallowed and suddenly sat down in the big blue velvet chair. "That's a lot for a woman to live up to."

"You'd be a tough act to replace, that's for sure," he said, not bothering to clear the huskiness from his tone.

Her gaze shied away from his. The action gave him some consolation. It was nice to know the attraction between them wasn't just one-sided.

Yet, neither did it change anything.

There was still the contract.

She suddenly got to her feet and started pacing around the room. "Have you thought about when we should tell the kids about the baby?"

He unlocked his fingers. "I hadn't given it much thought. Have you?"

"We should probably tell them soon. I'm already having trouble buttoning my jeans."

He eyed her shape that was hidden underneath a loose sweater and a pair of black jeans. The bulk of the knit camouflaged her figure well. "We can tell them tonight if you'd like."

She ran her palm along the edge of the file cabinet and played with the handles. "I'll need to buy some maternity clothes. I might need to borrow some money from you until I can earn some extra."

It was only the sight of her poker-straight posture and the realization of her tension that kept his temper under control. "I'll pay for the clothes."

"I don't—"

"This pregnancy was created by both of us. You'll carry the baby and I'll pick up the tab." Then he tried to defuse the atmosphere so she'd be less resistant. "Mother Nature made the rules. Not me."

"I guess that's the only argument I can't win, isn't it?" Her color was high.

"You'll look a lot better pregnant than I would."

"You think so?" She tilted her head as if contemplating what he might look like. "I bet you'd be incredibly sexy."

He didn't trust the sudden devilry dancing in those blue eyes. "Did that doctor prescribe a hallucinatory drug?"

She licked her lips. "I have a very good imagination."

"I don't think I want to hear this."

If anything, her expression became naughtier. "You could probably get on the cover of *Vogue* magazine."

"You think so?" Without thinking, he started toward her.

The blues of her eyes widened, creating a brilliance that was mesmerizing. She took a step back and then stopped. Lifting her chin up high, she gave him a look that warned him not to come any closer.

Yet, he did, anyway. There was no turning back. He had to touch her or go insane.

When he was only a breath away, he lifted his hand

and drew his fingers along the creamy fineness of her cheek. Just one touch. That's all he'd allow himself.

It should have been enough.

It wasn't. The mere brushing of his flesh against hers nearly brought him to his knees. He'd forgotten how perfect she felt.

Or had he?

In the wee hours of morning, with Hulk taking half the couch and Princess pressed close, it was memories of Abby that dominated his senses. No matter how many positions he tried to arrange himself in on that lumpy couch, or how many times he tried to push the dog and cat away from him, he couldn't forget the taste of Abby. Or her scent. Or the throaty cries she emitted when they made love.

Touching her brought to life every moment they were together.

"I don't think this is a good idea." Her voice was barely above a whisper.

The plea tugged at him. He wanted to pretend he didn't hear her. In the mirrors of her eyes, he knew she wasn't unaffected by his callused fingertips. With very little resistance she would come willingly into his arms and they could re-create the passion between them. The temptation beckoned. His arms were heavy with need.

But afterward...

It took every ounce of strength he had to step away and let his hand drop back to his side.

Abby's sigh sounded like a mixture of regret and relief. He kept his own pain locked inside, knowing he had doomed himself to another long night. The ticking clock was the only intrusion to the quiet filling the room.

She swallowed, the action telling of her own strain.

Had she been caught in that maze of hoping he'd ignore her request? He wanted to demand the answer.

Yeah, but what good would it do? He'd made her a promise. If this marriage was going to work, he had to be the one person whose word she could trust.

Abby brushed back her hair. "I'm sorry."

"Don't be." He didn't sound like himself. Hardly surprising. He didn't feel like himself, either.

"It doesn't seem to get any easier, does it?"

He shook his head. He'd exhausted his limited vocabulary.

She stepped back and looked away from him. "I'll start on the books tomorrow."

As she turned and left the room, a wake of emptiness lapped over him. He forced himself to stay where he was. If he moved, he'd have gone after her and tried to persuade her to stay.

Neither of them wanted that.

This marriage was supposed to have been so simple and straightforward. Their individual problems were to be solved by it.

What he hadn't foreseen was the problems their marriage had unleashed.

The pregnancy, Jason's attitude and Paige sleeping in his bed were issues they could deal with. Devlin hadn't expected perfection. That would have been unrealistic. And if nothing else, he was a realist.

The problem that was suddenly looming larger before him, growing with each day that passed, was the urge to make this marriage real in every sense of the word.

It wasn't just because they'd created a new life between them.

He wanted Abby because she was Abby. Not only because she was his wife. Not only because she was going to have his baby.

He liked the idea of Abby having his baby. Nothing could please him more. But not like this. He wanted to share the bounty of this moment as any normal husband would. He wanted to bring his wife crackers in bed. Drive out for a midnight snack, if that's what she craved. This baby should be a natural extension of a normal marriage relationship. But he knew that wouldn't happen. Abby would never ask. She would never expect those kinds of things from him.

He knew that as certainly as he knew his name.

Abby had learned not to depend. Not become dependent. In the past, that knowledge had protected her from being hurt when she was forced to leave one situation and move to another.

She had survived and become stronger.

He had no business asking for her vulnerability.

But he wanted it. Hungered for it. Desired it on the most basic level a man could feel.

And for a brief moment, he almost demanded she give it.

Touching her had been a potent combination of heaven and hell. He'd wanted to sweep her off her feet and carry her into the bedroom. The scent of her lingered, playing havoc with his libido. It had been hell to forgo the temptation.

It would be hell trying to forget.

Chapter Five

On the home front, nothing changed.

Devlin chopped more wood. He built four floor-to-ceiling bookshelves, which now held all Abby's cookbooks and then some.

The night after their conversation in his study, he and Abby together had told the kids about the baby.

Paige had clapped her hands and pronounced in no uncertain terms that she wanted a baby sister. She had promptly started picking out names. Each day was something different. So far, the baby in her mommy's tummy had been called Baby Jenny, Baby Sally, Baby Betsy and Baby Kelly. Kelly was in honor of Kelly Castner, her "bestest friend in the whole world."

Jason's reaction was fairly predictable. With his eyelids lowered to half-mast, he snorted with derision and stalked back into his room.

His oldest son's reaction hadn't surprised Devlin. Wrapped up in their own rock-and-roll universes, teenagers preferred to pretend they didn't have brothers and sisters, period. Neither did they like to believe their parents had sex.

Despite Jason's indifference, Devlin figured the baby would break down Jason's defenses just as Paige had. Little Paige had pretty much wrapped her big brother around her finger. All she had to do was bat her baby blues and Jase was putty in her hands. He kept his bedroom door shut against the rest of the world except for his stepsister, who could come and go as she liked. Paige had discovered what Jason would prefer the world not to know—he was a softie.

The baby would figure it out, too.

Riley was a different matter entirely. His reaction to the news had been to give no reaction at all.

Of the three children, his youngest son had embraced this new family arrangement with unabashed eagerness. Riley followed Abby around like a happy puppy. And not once since Devlin's marriage to Abby had the teacher or principal called to report any incidents at school. No fights. No stealing of schoolbags. No pulling of hair. Obviously, Abby had been the answer to his youngest son's problems.

If Riley was threatened by the baby, he wasn't telling. He hadn't asked any questions or argued with Paige whether the baby might be a boy or a girl. If Devlin didn't know better, he'd wonder if Riley had even heard what was said.

Devlin decided to take the wait-and-see approach. Riley couldn't keep anything bottled up for long. He just hoped his son spilled his feelings soon. It wasn't healthy to build up frustrations.

And he, more than anyone, knew that kind of pain.

He was finding it harder and harder each day to keep his feelings for Abby in check.

It didn't help that his parents were crazy about her, singing her praises and patting his back for marrying such a wonderful woman. His mother had invited them over for several meals and had been thrilled each time Abby brought along one of her cookbooks to lend to her. His dad wasn't any less enthusiastic, slapping his knee with delight when Abby encouraged him to tell several of his old "war" stories.

While Devlin was pleased that his wife and his parents got along, he wished he could share a little of their comfort level.

Having Abby in the house meant that her presence was stamped everywhere. She'd added the little touches to the house that he'd never thought to add. There was a mirror in the downstairs bathroom. There were now knick-knacky-type things sitting on end tables and window ledges. She'd even gotten rid of the plastic place mats and paper napkins, replacing them with a flowery table-cloth and real napkins.

Now that Abby had taken over the bookkeeping in his office, he couldn't hibernate there in the evenings. Being in the same room with her and not being able to touch her produced a perpetual state of agony.

Even when he wasn't in the same room with her, he couldn't escape being aware of Abby. Especially not after he pulled open his underwear drawer one day and realized she'd folded his briefs. He and the boys usually just emptied the laundry basket right into the drawers. They didn't even have to touch their clothes from the moment they left the basket until they had to wear them.

But Abby folded *his* underwear.

And wearing his underwear hadn't been the same since.

Who'd ever believed hell could be so damn hot?

* * *

The next afternoon at exactly 12:58 p.m., Abby decided there had to be something wrong with her. She'd caught herself daydreaming again when she should have been perusing the cookbook in front of her and planning dinner for the family. Normally, she was a very focused person. Concentration came easily for her. Yet, lately, her ability to concentrate had been thrown off kilter. Something was shorting out her brain circuits. Or rather, someone.

Devlin Hamilton.

It wasn't natural for a pregnant woman to be obsessed with her husband, was it?

For the sake of the family, she had to gain control over her erratic—and sometimes erotic—tendencies. Her marriage to Devlin was, in essence, a professional relationship. Nothing more. Nothing less. Devlin was her partner in this venture and deserved her respect and adherence to the agreement between them.

Looking at the cookbook in front of her, she admitted to herself that he also deserved more than eggs.

She closed the cookbook and went up to the bedroom. Pulling down her old beat-up suitcase from the closet shelf, she reached into an invisible slit on the side and pulled out a well-worn manila envelope. Then she replaced the suitcase, and headed out the door, tapping the envelope against her hand while reviewing her options and plan of attack.

There wasn't much in life she considered herself to be an expert on. Certainly she was no expert when it came to understanding men and to conducting a marriage. Even trying to read Devlin and understand what was going on between them made her stomach twist into knots. She couldn't begin to make sense of her reaction to him.

For the well-being of her sanity, she set her mind to what she did know.

In particular, she knew teenagers because she'd been there. Crazed hormones, making the transition between tomboy clothes to training bras, blocking out the advice of those who deemed themselves older but wiser and tuning in rock-and-roll heroes who had suddenly become gods. She remembered every agonizing, exhilarating year and figured she could use her the-world-is-against-me knowledge to tackle the job ahead of her. Those formative years were the ones most firmly entrenched in her memory.

By her estimation, the timing was right.

Ever since her arrival, Jason had maintained a wary distance, living on the fringes. He showed up at mealtime, ate just enough to get by so he didn't earn a reprimand from his father, and disappeared immediately to the never-never land of his room. He communicated mostly with Paige and Riley. Paige, because she pestered him until he gave in, and Riley so he had someone to argue with. Other than responding to his father's questions, he didn't go out of his way to be a part of the family. Abby pretended not to notice. He was a teenager, and teenagers existed in a different world.

But he was also a member of the family, and he had a skill the family needed.

From everything she'd learned, Jason could cook. Although she'd never tasted his culinary efforts, others had. Even Rebecca Castner had mentioned to her that Jason was something of a genius when it came to the kitchen domain. She'd found late-night pots and pans in the stainless-steel sink more than once, so she figured Jason wouldn't mind taking over the cooking. However, he had to want to do it. She didn't want to take away his enjoyment.

That called for a strategic presentation of her plan. A smart teenager like Jason would be on the lookout for any sign of manipulation or trickery. He would have to be convinced this was what he wanted.

Instead of shutting himself in his room before mealtime, she had a feeling he'd prefer to be the cook-in-charge. She was more than willing to bestow that honor, and she'd taken her time setting the stage. He had to be getting itchy to take over. Her egg combinations were going from bad to worse—partly by intention.

Still, timing and execution were crucial.

At three thirty-five on the dot, Jason walked into the house. His uncovered ears brutally red from the freezing cold, he wore an old army coat, baggy pants and heavy hiking boots.

"Hi, Jason," she greeted him as he walked past her into the kitchen.

"Hi." As usual, his tone was guarded.

"How was school?"

"Fine," came his standard response.

She waited until after he'd grabbed an ice-cream sandwich from the freezer and retreated to his room. His routine never changed. Same tone. Same number of strides to the kitchen and back. Same closing of the bedroom door.

So far so good. Everything was on schedule.

She watched the clock, gauging the time it would take for him to finish the treat, crumple the paper, pace the floor to the wastebasket and throw the wrapping into the trash. Then she took her position in front of his room. It was imperative she grab his attention before he donned his headphones and shut out the rest of the world.

Rapping briskly on his bedroom door, she heard the bed squeak, then silence. That was a good sign. At least he hadn't turned on his music yet. She raised her knuckles to the wood surface again. This time, before she could perform more than one knock, the door swung open.

A slightly hostile expression dragged down his eyebrows, producing a shroud of suspicion. "Yeah?"

She ignored the lack of cordiality and went straight to the heart of the matter. "I want to make a trade."

His eyelids descended to half-mast. "A trade?"

"You know. I give you something and you give me something in return."

"What is it?"

"Can I come in?" She had him, whether he knew it or not. If he'd closed the door in her face, she would have been back to square one. That would have presented a big problem because it would have put him on guard and neither of them would get what they wanted. She didn't mind begging. But respect could only be gained among equals. It was a rule she'd learned years ago.

Jason took a moment to decide, but he finally shrugged and moved aside.

Abby walked into the middle of the room, stepping without comment over an untidy pile of clothes and several pairs of sneakers.

Turning, she met his gaze head-on.

The defensive posture of his stance and the slight upward angle of his chin told her he expected her to complain about the state of the room. She didn't. She wouldn't. One thing she'd learned during her bumpy travels through the foster-care system was how to go after what she wanted. She was here to bargain in good faith, not to cast judgment.

She offered him the large manila envelope she'd brought with her.

He made no move to take the envelope. "What is it?"

"You'll never know until you open it."

She kept her pose nonchalant as he took the packet from her hand, his motions slow and reluctant.

Reaching into the well-worn, golden packet, he pulled out a large eight-by-ten photo. For a moment, he didn't say a word as surprise lifted his expression. Without removing his gaze from the picture in his hand, he cleared his throat. "It's James Dean. You have an autographed picture of James Dean? Where did you get it? Did you know James Dean?"

The reverence in his voice told her everything she wanted to know. She'd been right. Ever since she'd put the clean laundry in his room and discovered he had three full-size posters of the fifties rebel hanging in his room, she'd known the old picture would be her bargaining chip.

Taking her time, she sat down on the chair next to his desk before answering his question.

She decided there would be nothing gained by pointing out the fact that she wasn't even born when his hero was killed. In Jason's eyes, she belonged to the "old" generation. "I wish I had." She sighed, an echo of her youthful obsession with the star.

Jason didn't appear convinced. "How do you know it's James Dean's real signature?"

"My foster father was an extra in one of Dean's last movies."

"Cool."

"Yeah."

He swallowed and touched the corners of the picture

almost reverently. "How come you didn't ever frame it?"

Questions about her past were not her favorite topic of discussion. Yet, she knew Jason wouldn't respect anything but the truth. "When you're a foster child, you don't always get to keep what is yours. You never know what will be taken or get left behind when you move on." Or stolen. She chose not to point out that reality, however. "I didn't want anyone else knowing I had it. No one paid much attention to the envelope. So that's where I kept it. Then I'd pull the picture out whenever I wanted to see him."

Jason finally glanced up. For once, his expression didn't carry any animosity or hide any secrets. "You didn't have a real family?"

"My parents were killed when I was very young."

"That's tough."

She gave him a half smile. "For some kids, that's life."

The wariness returned to his face. She could see the doubts flitting through his mind. She didn't push. Just let him absorb, and reach his own conclusions. Nothing teenagers hated more than to have an adult make decisions for them.

Finally, the boy asked, "Why are you giving the picture to me?"

She couldn't risk sounding too eager. "I understand you're a pretty decent cook."

His face turned a bit red as he shuffled his feet. "It's no big deal."

"It is if the only thing you can cook is eggs," she said with ample self-deprecation.

For a sliver of a second, the corners of his mouth tweaked as a smile fought to break free. Then he donned his familiar expression of indifference again. "Eggs are okay."

"For chickens," she drawled.

His gaze gleamed, reminding her of his father's. "Snakes are hatched from them, too."

She didn't have to feign her shudder. "How could I forget?"

He snickered out loud before he brought up a hand and tried to cover his laughter with a cough.

Abby had to make sure he didn't see the soft smile she was holding inside. Jason Hamilton was a neat kid. "So how about it?"

"How about what?"

"I give you the picture and you give me some guidance in the kitchen?"

He eyed her skeptically. "Hasn't anyone ever taught you how to cook before?"

The kid was smart, too. "They tried but I flunked every single course they tried to teach me."

"You going to serve eggs again tonight?"

"Do you like them with sweet-and-sour sauce?"

He turned a little green. "You can set the table. I'll cook."

She made sure to keep her face averted so her stepson wouldn't catch sight of her satisfaction. "Thanks, Jason."

She stood up and started toward the door, when his voice stopped her. "Abby, you don't have to give me the picture."

She turned as he thrust the envelope and picture toward her. "You don't want it?"

He shrugged. "I like to cook. It's not that big of a deal. You don't need to give up the picture." His words said one thing, his eyes told her something different.

One of the hardest things she ever had to do was to stay on her side of the room and to keep from blowing everything she'd gained by wrapping him in her arms.

She hadn't dared hope for more than she'd come for, but he'd just given her a gift that was more valuable than all the gold in Fort Knox. She knew he wanted that picture. The fact that he was willing to give her what she wanted without taking James Dean in return brought tears to her eyes. She looked down at her shoes, allowing her hair to slip forward and conceal her emotion. Blinking back the moisture, she pushed the envelope toward him. "Whatever. It's yours if you want. I don't need it anymore."

"Why not?"

With a steadiness she didn't feel, she said, "That picture was all I had when I was your age. It brought me happiness. But now I have you, Riley, your dad and Paige. That's all I ever wanted. If you'll do the cooking, then everybody will be happy. And that's what I want now. My family's happiness."

She didn't wait for him to answer. She wasn't about to push her luck.

Chapter Six

Abby's sense of satisfaction didn't last long. The next day, she had just finished two loads of laundry and was reflecting on the rave reviews that Jason had earned the night before after he served spaghetti, when the sudden shrill of the phone broke into her thoughts.

She picked up the receiver. "Hello?"

"Mrs. Hamilton?"

The use of her married name made her hesitate for a second. She still wasn't used to hearing her new title. "Yes, this is Mrs. Hamilton."

"This is Mrs. Branson from the Humphrey Elementary School. I'm Riley's teacher. I tried to page your husband an hour ago but he didn't return my call."

Abby's hand tightened around the receiver. "Is something wrong?"

The pause told its own story. "Riley and another boy got into a fight at school." The regret in the teacher's voice was clear even through the phone lines. "We have a policy that when something like this happens, a parent needs to come to school and take the child home. Since this isn't Riley's first infraction, the principal is considering suspending him for two days."

Before the teacher had finished, Abby reached for her purse. "I'll be there as soon as I can."

During the entire trip home, Riley sat in the passenger seat and stared silently out the window. Despite his hair rioting in a few more directions than usual, on the surface, he appeared none the worse for wear. Yet, his unnatural stillness was a stark contrast to the energetic, talkative boy who usually had trouble finding enough time to breathe between words.

He wouldn't look her straight in the eye when she picked him up; another unusual tactic for Riley.

As soon as they walked into the house, Abby took a closer look at his face. She noticed the puffiness to the right corner of his face. "That eye is going to be an interesting shade in the morning," she commented without a hint of judgment. "Why don't you go clean your face and then we'll put an ice pack on your eye."

His gaze darted to her and then shifted away again. "It doesn't hurt. Maybe I should go lie down."

"Are you feeling ill?"

He shook his head, his freckles standing out like soldiers at attention.

"Go get the washcloth and then we'll talk," she said softly, giving him a slight push toward the bathroom.

He shuffled away and took as long as he could to wash his face. Finally, he returned to the living room. "Can we talk in my bedroom?"

She followed him into his small room.

He walked over to the bed and she sat down next to him. "Do you want to tell me what happened?"

He shrugged. "Bobby and I aren't friends anymore."

Bobby Carmichael was his best buddy. "Why not?"

Riley didn't answer.

"Did you have an argument?" she asked.

Riley picked up his baseball glove and fidgeted with the ties. "He said something I didn't like."

"Do you want to talk about it?"

"No."

She'd never seen anyone look more miserable in his life than the small boy sitting next to her. She chewed on her lip a bit and considered how to help Riley get the load off his chest. Whatever was bothering him might be part of the quietness she'd noticed the past few days. Ever since he'd learned that he was going to have a new brother or sister, he'd been prone to bouts of silence—a very unRiley-like trait. One minute he'd be almost hysterical with laughter. The next he would be moody.

Was this fight with Bobby another part of the pattern?

"I thought Bobby was your friend."

"Not anymore." Riley tossed away the glove and scuffed the toe of his shoe against the floor.

"Why not?"

"Because he's dumb."

Abby saw the hurt behind the bitter denouncement. She reached down and picked up the glove and placed it on the dresser next to the bed. "You don't really believe that, do you?"

A loud sniff gave testimony to the battle being waged inside the boy. For a moment, Abby despaired he'd hold on to the pain.

Then the dam burst, and a big tear rolled down his face. "He said you weren't my real mom." He dashed the back of his hand angrily against his cheek. "He said you were just a pretend mom."

As a second tear began its pilgrimage down the other side of his cheek, Abby leaned over and tenderly brushed it away with the pad of her thumb. Lifting his chin, she made him look straight into her eyes. "I don't think it's important what Bobby thinks. It's only important what you think."

He didn't blink. "My real mom didn't want me."

The baldness of his statement couldn't be backed away from. If only there were a magic cure for heartache. For rejection. For abandonment. Kids shouldn't have to be hurt by the actions of grown-ups. Yet, that, too, was a reality. She knew Riley was asking questions she didn't have answers to. His pain couldn't be soothed or healed. He didn't need her anger or any glib answers. The only true gift she could give him was the permission to talk about the hurt. Lay it open and tell him it was okay to be angry and hurt.

She chose her words with care. "Your mother wouldn't have given birth to you if she didn't want you."

He pulled his chin out of her hand and clenched his fist. "Why doesn't she ever call or come to see us?"

How many times had she wondered why all her foster families seemed to forget her so easily after she left?

She'd vowed that Paige would never feel that sense of isolation or abandonment.

Riley needed the same commitment. Even though she didn't know what the future held, she knew she would never abandon this young boy. He needed her.

Her arms ached with the need to hold him, but she didn't think he was ready for that yet. "I don't know why your mother left. Maybe someday you can ask her. But one thing you know is before she left, she made sure you had a good home and a good dad to watch over you. That's more than some children ever have."

Riley swallowed, his gaze never leaving Abby's. His face was alive with the inner conflict taking place. He sniffed. "She's never sent me a birthday present."

If his real mother could see him now, would she regret the choices she made? Abby had to struggle with her own anger against the woman she didn't know. But her anger wouldn't help Riley. Hate destroyed. Love healed.

Abby gave in to temptation and tried to smooth one of his stubborn, wayward curls. "When is your birthday?"

"November fifth."

"Did you do anything special?"

A hint of a smile came to his face. "Dad let me invite all of my friends to a pizza party."

"Did you have it here?"

He shook his head. "We did last year. But Willie Gross broke the bathroom window, and Lionel spilled juice all over the couch. Dad said he'd let the pizza people clean up the mess from now on."

Abby nearly smiled at the thought of Devlin on his knees, cursing a stain. "You have a special dad."

"Yeah."

"He made sure you had a party even though he didn't like cleaning up the mess. Not everybody has a dad like that."

Riley nodded. "Fred Stangler's dad is real grumpy. He's always yellin' and stuff."

She didn't interrupt as Riley made his own connections and conclusions. She knew this wouldn't end his questions about his mother's desertion. It wouldn't completely take away the hurt, either, but at least he'd found a way to vent his hurt without taking a poke at Bobby. That was a positive sign.

He picked up his glove and plucked at the laces again. "Fred doesn't even have a big brother like Jason."

"Did Jason give you your baseball glove?"

He nodded. "He gave it to me for my birthday. It's better than the one Bobby has."

"Does he have a brother?"

"Just a little one. Bobby says he's a real little stinker. He gets into his stuff all the time."

"I bet he wishes he had a big brother like yours who could teach him how to play ball."

Riley's tears had almost disappeared. "I guess so. Jason is cool sometimes, when he isn't too crabby." Then he tilted his head and eyed her. "I have a dad, a brother, a stepmom and a stepsister. That's a lot, isn't it?"

"Yes, it is." She let him absorb this thought before casually adding, "And soon you'll have a new baby brother or sister. That's another person to love."

"Yeah." A frown settled amongst his freckles as he released her gaze and studied his glove. He shifted restlessly on the bed.

Abby knew better than to expect a miracle but decided to give him something to think about. "This baby will be lucky to have you as a big brother."

His head came up again. "It will?"

"You'll be able to teach him or her to play baseball. Big brothers are important."

Riley didn't look convinced. "Did your big brother teach you to play baseball, too?"

"I didn't have any brothers or sisters."

"Not any?"

"No."

"So you didn't have to share your toys or your mom and dad with anyone else?" The note of envy was unmistakable.

She shook her head. "I didn't have a mom and dad, either."

The envy disappeared from the small boy's face. His eyes grew wide with distress. "Didn't anyone buy you presents or give you a birthday party, either?"

To a kid, getting presents was almost as important as breathing. Abby didn't want Riley to worry about something that happened a long time ago. "I didn't have any birthday parties, but someone usually gave me a present for my birthday." She put a finger on his freckled nose. "What would you like to do for your birthday next year?"

He shrugged. "I dunno. Maybe go to Benny's again for pizza. That way, you and Dad won't have to scrub the couch."

She struggled not to smile. "You can start thinking about it and let me know when the time gets closer."

"Okay." He seemed unusually sober again.

Pursing his lips, he got to his feet and scuffled around the room. Abby waited as he picked up a toy soldier, moved the arms, bent the head forward and set it down again. Then he flipped through a book, not actually looking at the pages. Finally, he turned and slid her a cautious glance. "Maybe it would be okay if I called you Mom? Just sometimes. Not always. It might be easier."

Her own tears were just a heartbeat away, but she willed them under control. "I'd be honored if you called me Mom anytime it feels right for you."

A smile as brilliant as the Fourth of July broke out across Riley's face. "I think I might feel like doing it a lot—" he paused, then added "—Mom."

She rose to her feet and gave him a quick hug, brief and to the point. Just as quickly, and before he suffered too much embarrassment, she released him and headed for the door. When she reached the doorway, she looked back at him and waved a motherly finger at him. "And no more fights at school. Are we clear on that?"

"Yes, Mom." The statement accompanied a wide grin.

Devlin removed himself from the doorway so Abby and Riley wouldn't think he was spying on them.

He'd finally gotten the message from Riley's teacher and learned Abby had retrieved his son from school.

Upon arriving home, he'd followed the trail of voices to Riley's room.

His urge to throttle Riley and ground him for the rest of the school year had dissipated as soon as he picked up the thread of discussion between Abby and Riley. What became immediately apparent to him was Abby's intuitiveness about what was really bothering Riley.

Not once had he associated Riley's school shenanigans with Linda. Why hadn't he realized that Riley might be questioning his real mother's desertion?

Riley had been a baby when Linda had left and they'd divorced. His youngest son only knew his mother from a few photos that Jason had sitting in his room. Devlin didn't recall Riley asking why she didn't send him presents for his birthday or why Linda left or if she was ever coming to visit.

Or had he?

Maybe Riley had been asking all along but Devlin didn't understand the message. How long had this been bothering Riley? Why hadn't his son come to him?

Abby rounded the corner into the living room. She stopped as she caught sight of him. "I didn't realize you were home."

"I didn't think it was a good idea to interrupt."

"So you heard?"

He nodded. "I guess I should have realized he'd have questions about his mother."

He raked a hand through his hair, making deep ridges.

Abby sat down on the edge of the large sofa as Devlin claimed the middle of the cushions. "I'm not sure Riley knew exactly what was bothering him. He only knew something didn't feel right."

"He recognized them with you."

She shook her head. "It's the baby. He's afraid of being ignored or forgotten."

He frowned. "Is that what this is about?"

She got to her feet and walked around the couch to stand behind him. Placing her hands on his shoulders, she began to massage the hard ridge of muscle.

His body went on red alert beneath her fingertips, tensing and straining. He forgot to breathe. She stopped. "Does this bother you?"

Yeah, it bothered him, all right. Everything about her bothered him. But not in the way she meant. He was fighting every basic urge known to man not to pull her over the edge of the sofa and sweep her into his arms. His body swam with desire, so hard, so needy, he wanted to sell his soul. "No, it feels good. You just surprised me."

After a brief hesitation, she continued kneading his neck muscles. "How much contact has Riley had with his real mother?"

"None."

His blunt response brought a momentary pause then she resumed. "I see."

He was beginning to realize Abby saw a lot more than he ever did. "Thanks for talking to him. For not making excuses for his mother or destroying any fantasies, either.

Linda doesn't deserve any kind of motherhood awards. But someday…'' He let his voice trail off.

She finished the rest of his thought. "Someday she's going to regret not knowing who her sons are and the boys will both have a lot of things to overcome before they can mend. Is that what you meant?"

The muscles in his neck were absorbing and reveling in the magic of her touch. It would take a nuclear war to make him move from his spot. "Anyone ever tell you that you are a very smart woman, Abby Hamilton?"

He felt her tremble.

"I'm not sure that I'm any smarter than anyone else. But I learned a few lessons along the way."

"You know what it's like to be without a parent. No one else could give him that kind of reassurance. Only you."

Devlin quit fighting his desires and went by pure instinct. He turned and pulled Abby around the edge of the couch and into his lap. She didn't resist.

The blue of her gaze deepened and met his. He didn't hide his need. Using the pad of his finger against the satin of her skin, he caressed the creamy texture, watching a blush fan across the pale surface and spread to her neck. Moving downward, he found the sexy indentation of her dimple before moving over to trace the gentle curve of her mouth. He heard her breath quicken and saw her eyes dilate.

Her tongue poked out and wet the surface on her mouth. "You don't need to thank me. That's part of my job."

He shook his head. "You could have grounded Riley. Threatened him with a week of bread and water—"

"He might have preferred that to eggs every night."

He ignored her attempt to make light of her role in

getting his son to unburden himself. "Or you could have sent him to his room and left him there to contemplate the error of his ways. You didn't have to take the time to listen and discover what's going on in his six-year-old head. It would have been easier to shut the door."

She worried the corner of her lip unconsciously. "Those things wouldn't have solved anything. He still would have been hurting and he would have just acted out his frustrations again."

He stroked the corner of her lip where her teeth had left their mark. "You saved both of us a lot of aggravation and heartache."

"I'm here to make your life easier." The honeyed warmth of her tone tugged at his insides, making each word ooze with sex appeal.

"Easier" wasn't what she was doing to his life, he thought as he contemplated her eyes turning into the color of Lake Michigan. The color had never intrigued him before. It did now.

"Dad?"

Riley's voice in the doorway cut through Devlin's self-absorption. Without taking his eyes from Abby, Devlin said, "Aren't you supposed to be in your room studying?"

"They don't give us much homework in the first grade."

Devlin gestured toward the door. "Then find something else to do."

"Okay." The eagerness in Riley's voice seemed at odds with the request, but Devlin wasn't about to question it. Right now, he wanted his son to leave the room so he could continue his contemplation of Abby.

As Riley left, a dimple quirked in Abby's cheek. "He sounded awfully happy to be doing schoolwork."

"Let's count our blessings."

"That seems wise."

"Abby?" Riley's voice came through the doorway before he reappeared in the room.

The groove in Abby's cheek deepened at the sound of Riley's voice. The suppressed merriment in her face invited Devlin to share the humor. "Yes, Riley?"

"Do we have any bananas?"

"I think there are some in the pantry." She looked past Devlin's shoulder to the boy. "Do you want me to cut one up for you?"

"Nope. I can do it."

As soon as he left again, Abby turned to Devlin. "Do you suppose we should make sure he doesn't cut his finger off?"

He shook his head. The last thing he wanted to do was worry about Riley. "I've hidden all the sharp knives."

"You are a wise father, Devlin Hamilton."

"I married you, didn't I?"

His teasing evoked a flush that worked up past the collar of her shirt and blossomed across her skin. He saw the way she tried to hold herself still, as if unaffected by his nearness. The slight tremble of her lips and the skittered pattern to her breathing told him the truth. She was as aware of him as he was of her.

But how aware?

He suddenly needed to know the answer. A quick taste of her lips would surely solve the mystery.

Don't be a fool, Hamilton. Remember what happened the last time, a voice inside his head warned.

Heck, he remembered, all right. There wasn't a moment that had passed since their wedding night when he didn't remember. Maybe if he purged the memory from his mind, he could forget. The idea had merit. Now all he had to do was figure out what it would take to forget fireworks and passion so intense that it had stenciled itself permanently into his brain. A kiss might do it. Of course, it couldn't be an ordinary one. But then he doubted any kiss with Abby could ever be classified as ordinary. Nope. It would have to be thoroughly transacted. Something to take the edge off his hunger once and for all.

That's all he'd take.

Then he'd be satisfied. He could sleep again, and he wouldn't be so damn hungry all the time.

The longer he stared into her crystal-pool gaze, the more he was convinced he'd reached the only solution to his ongoing dilemma. The fact that she hadn't moved away from him seemed to rubber-stamp the decision.

Before he could question his conclusions, he lifted his hands to Abby's face. Her startled jerk didn't stop him as he cupped her jaw. Her hands came instinctively toward him. Whether to push him away or pull him to her, he didn't know. It wouldn't have mattered. They both needed to put their wedding night behind them. Surely she didn't want this tension any more than he did. This kiss would extinguish the craziness and put them back on track.

He had to believe that.

Then logic deserted him.

Like a starving man who had just stumbled onto a lush oasis, he followed his instincts and moved to quench his gut-wrenching thirst for her lips. A man couldn't go without water for too many days. He needed a sip to replenish himself. That was all. He wouldn't ask for more. Above all things he was a man of his word.

"Abby," he breathed just before he staked his claim.

"Devlin." His name sounded like a plea.

His lips moved in and covered hers. He told himself that if he could just touch her, then it would be enough.

Her hands fluttered against his chest, but when a growl of hunger rose from deep inside of him, any resistance she might have had evaporated as she grabbed a shirtful of cloth and clutched him closer to her.

His dreams didn't do her justice. Abby tasted sweeter and hotter than he remembered. The kiss didn't pretend or flirt. It was blatantly honest. He gave. She answered and gave back with a generosity that was so perfectly Abby.

How had he resisted this woman so long?

Why had he tried?

The simmering heat in his veins broke into flame. The woman was a powder keg. She didn't flirt. She didn't pretend to be coy. Or try to be cute. If she had been, he might have been cured of the fever burning in him. Instead, she seduced him with honesty and raw need. The desire within her hit him with a force he craved.

Life began with the moment he took her in his arms. Time lost its beat and became unending.

Nothing else mattered.

Then he became aware of Abby's hands suddenly coming between them.

She tore her lips from him and the kiss came to an abrupt end. "Wait." Her shoulders heaved as she gasped for air to replenish her lungs. "Aren't we supposed to breathe or something?"

"Not if we don't have to," he growled, reaching for her again.

Riley's voice stopped him. "Dad, can I use your razor to shave my head?"

Chapter Seven

Devlin, still reeling from the devastating impact of kissing Abby, had trouble translating Riley's question.

Jason, who had apparently arrived home from school without their hearing him, followed his younger brother into the room. "Why do you want to shave your head, squirt?"

Riley shrugged. "You told me all the babes are hot for Michael Jordan because he shaved his head. If I shave mine, the babes will be hot for me." He used his hand to flatten down his red curls. "What do you think?"

"You look like a dork," was his big brother's response.

Devlin noticed how hard Abby was working to hold back her laughter. "Babes?" he asked his oldest son.

Jason hitched a thumb in his front pants pocket and shifted to a defensive posture. "It's just guy talk. I can't help it that he listens to my phone calls."

Devlin didn't know what was harder to do. Regroup after kissing Abby or digest the knowledge that his six-year-old son was trying to attract *babes.* "That's no excuse for referring to women as babes."

Jason produced a rude sound. "I didn't mean nothin' by it."

He left the room before he received any more lectures.

Riley looked at them with uncertainty. "Does this mean I can't shave my head?"

"That's right. It also means you get to sweep the kitchen and pantry, plus do the dishes tonight since you were sent home early from school again."

"But, Dad—"

"And the longer it takes you to get started, the more things I'll add to the list."

Riley's mouth clamped shut as he stomped out of the room before another word was said.

He'd barely left, when Abby let go of her laughter. She laughed so hard, tears rolled down her face.

Devlin pulled his handkerchief from his back pocket and handed it to her to wipe away her tears. "Would you believe Riley didn't come with a warning label when he arrived in this world?"

"Apparently, Congress hasn't tackled that regulation yet." She dabbed her eyes and returned his handkerchief. "He's a normal, curious six-year-old."

"Is he? I don't remember Jason ever being quite so precocious."

"Maybe he was just better at hiding it or working things out for himself."

"Maybe."

She touched his arm. "Riley's curious about relationships. His curiosity isn't wrong. He's just trying to understand and find his own place." She removed her hand from his skin and stood up. "Would you really want him to be any different?"

"Not for one moment," he answered without hesitation.

"I didn't think so."

After she left the room, it wasn't the peculiarities behind Riley's precocious behavior that had Devlin in a tailspin. It was the questions and possible directions he could take in furthering his own relationship with his new wife that kept him sitting on the couch for another thirty minutes.

The kiss hadn't removed the memory of their wedding night. Instead, it had lit a new wick of desire. Fanned the need into a rampaging fire.

If he thought he wanted Abby before, it was nothing like the way he wanted her now.

Why in the heck had he ever signed that bloody contract?

Abby closed the door of Devlin's office behind her and sagged against the smooth wood panel. Her heart was still carrying on as if she'd just outrun a jaguar in the wilds of Africa. Perhaps she'd escaped from an animal twice as deadly.

Devlin?

No. It was her. One Abigail O'Reilly Hamilton.

She was a wild woman on the loose. Out of control. Driven by instincts she didn't even realize she had. Poor Devlin never had a chance. All he'd had to do was look in her direction and she'd thrown herself at him. What had he thought?

A mock headline flashed through her head. Abby of the Jungle Attacks Spouse. She shuddered and squeezed her eyes closed.

Why?

How could it have happened? She had always kept her

feet on the ground and her emotions under control. She'd known better than to believe in fairy dust and pots of gold at the other end of the rainbow. Her only mistake with her former husband had been to turn over her financial security to him. That had been stupid and she'd paid the price. Learned her lesson, too, or so she thought.

Maybe her hormones were out of whack. Pregnant women did have unusual cravings. Pickles and ice cream. Herring. Food was a logical obsession for a woman who would soon be the unapologetic size of a boatyard. Yet, she wasn't even tempted to raid the refrigerator in the middle of the night.

No, her obsession had sexy, green eyes that could make a woman forget all the lessons she'd learned. Both a peculiar desire and one that was all too ridiculous for a woman like her. She'd been married once before. There was no reason for stars to be in her eyes.

There had to be something wrong.

The doctor, however, had assured her that everything about this pregnancy was normal. Of course, she hadn't told him about her unusual cravings and her outrageous addictions. He'd think she was nuts.

What woman became tormented by desires for her husband?

No one that she ever knew.

Maybe there was something in the water up here in Wisconsin. Too much lead. Or iron. Or maybe her bra was too tight and had cut off circulation to key brain cells.

She shouldn't be so conscious of the way Devlin's clothes clung to his well-defined frame. Her gaze shouldn't be tracking his confident, long strides from across the room. And she certainly shouldn't be so intrigued by the cheek-to-cheek motion of his butt, for crying out loud. No, there'd been no way to bring this to the doctor's attention. Besides, how would you treat something like that? Was there a vitamin that could delete sexual fantasies?

No, probably not. Vitamins usually added something to one's support system. She needed some kind of dilution device. Perhaps she needed a laxative. Was there such a thing as an ex-sex laxative?

And even if there was, did she want it?

You're off your rocker, Abby, my girl.

PMS sidelined some women every month, but that malady never had made much of an impression on her moods. And except for that brief bout of morning sickness—which had thankfully disappeared—she'd hadn't had any problems with her pregnancy. All the signs were positive.

So why did she love to be in Devlin's office where his presence was stamped on everything from the basic file cabinet to the paper-peppered desk?

Pregnant and in heat. That's what she was. Perhaps she should go see a veterinarian instead.

Did Devlin suspect he'd married a madwoman? Given the way he hightailed it out of the house every evening to his workshop in the shed, she had the sinking feeling he probably did. The poor man probably feared she'd attack with lust or something.

Was she sending out waves?

She couldn't see her husband being scared of any woman. But maybe he'd suspected she was on the edge of becoming a clinging ninny. Is that what this was about? Maybe she was being too clingy. Maybe those old wants—intense desires to belong and to have what everyone else seemed to have and she didn't—were raising their jealous heads.

She'd have to deal with them. Batten them down so they didn't open up and expose her as desperate or weak. She knew what was expected of her. She had it in black and white. There was no question about her responsibilities, her duties or Devlin's expectations of her.

Abby sighed and opened her eyes just a crack and squinted at the file cabinet across the room. She should forget about her hiatus from sanity and get down to work. Adding figures was a good way to bring her hormones back in line.

It was a good device to help her stop thinking about Devlin and the kiss.

She could go through the invoices and write out the checks. They'd received the bonus for the project Devlin had finished several weeks ago and she needed to pay their subcontractors.

However, instead of pulling the business files from their respective drawers in the metal cabinet, she rifled through the manila folders and found the one headed Marriage Contract.

Slipping it free, she dragged out the contract she and Devlin had signed months ago. Scanning the official-looking contents, she muttered aloud the words that she already knew by heart. Nothing seemed any different. The ending statement read: *We agree to abide by this contract, unless one or both parties decides to terminate said marriage.*

At the time they signed it, she thought they'd covered everything they'd face. Now she knew differently. They hadn't addressed insanity, lust or obsessions.

Something that would explain the skittering of her nerves and lapse of control whenever Devlin was nearby. Something that would interpret the short circuitry of her common sense, defining why a calm and practical woman like her would toss aside every scrap of hard earned knowledge and indulge in behavior totally foreign to her.

What possible explanation could there be?

It wasn't as if she didn't have enough things to occupy her time. Boredom wasn't a part of her day. Doing the laundry for an active family of five wasn't any small feat. When Devlin came home from work, he donned a clean set of clothes after he showered. Jason, who played intramural basketball several times a week, also went through several changes of clothes a day. Whatever activities Riley and Paige participated in determined the state of their wardrobes, and Abby could usually count on tackling several stubborn stains per day generated by two children of that age. Those clothes, plus towels and bedding, meant she did two to three loads of wash every other day.

Then there was the cooking, the cleaning and the bookwork. Trying to stay on top of these duties, and the natural tiredness that went along with being pregnant made her well and truly tired by the time she crawled into bed each night.

She knew it wasn't idle hands that could account for her unnatural behavior.

While she'd never had much affection during the early years of her life—many times being quite lonely, in fact—all that loneliness had skedaddled the first time she held Paige in her arms. The overwhelming love for her daughter had filled all the empty places. Paige, a natural hugger, was as cuddly as cuddly could be.

Now there was Riley, who wanted to call her mother. Jason, who liked to pretend he didn't need her, but probably needed her the most.

And then there was the baby.

"Abby?"

She hadn't heard the door open but recognized the concern in Devlin's voice.

"It's the pregnancy," she blurted out before he could venture into the room.

He didn't come any farther into the room. "Pregnancy?"

"It's my hormones. They're out of whack."

His eyebrow lifted.

She couldn't think straight when his eyes turned that concerned shade of green. He probably was wondering if she'd need a straitjacket next. She rushed on, letting her tongue take the driver's seat while her brain sluggishly tried to catch up. "Some women crave pickles and ice cream. Others crave herring or liver. I, on the other hand, crave—" She stopped. Without having to look in a mirror, she knew a wave of ugly red had flooded her cheeks.

The devilish humor sprinting across Devlin's face made her shut her mouth with a snap.

"You were saying...?" he encouraged with a silky edge to his tone.

The feeling that she'd just made an absolute fool of herself provided the bracing she needed. She lifted her chin. "I'm sorry. I was thinking aloud. Did you need something?"

He waited a second or two for her to continue. When she didn't, he finally said, "Rebecca Castner called and invited us to their house on Friday night to get together and play games. Would that be okay with you?"

"What about the kids?"

"My mother has offered to take them for the weekend. They've been begging to show off their new granddaughter to their friends. It's a chance for them to spoil the kids when we're not looking."

Abby tried to think. If they were going to be alone for the weekend, she'd need a safe diversion. Getting together with the Castners seemed to be the ideal solution. "I'm not much of a game player."

"Neither am I." A killer smile of satisfaction gleamed at her. "That should be reassuring for both of us."

Reassurance was the last thing that Abby felt after Devlin left the room.

Later that night, Devlin sat in front of the big-screen television set without really seeing the play-by-play action of the basketball game.

Abby had been in his office for the past two hours, scrunched over the computer, logging numbers and muttering to herself. He'd tried to do some work, but having her nearby was a distraction. Time and time again, he'd find his gaze feasting on the creamy whiteness of her skin, the soft curl draped delicately behind the curve of her ear and the way she chewed absently on the fullness of her lip. He was continually fighting the urge to cross the room and drag her into his arms. The sweet memories of their wedding night tormented him more and more each day.

Then there was that kiss.

Sweet heaven, how was a man supposed to keep sane with that woman claiming every square inch of the house *and* his brain?

Not even the seesawing basketball game between the Bucks and Bulls could keep his mind off his wife. It seemed as if Abby's image filled his head whether he was swinging a hammer, measuring floor space or trying to sleep.

"Dad?"

From the impatient edge to Jason's voice, Devlin realized his son had been trying to get his attention.

Devlin straightened and pushed his fingers through his already mussed hair. "Sorry. Did you want to watch something different on TV? Go ahead and change the channel. This game isn't too exciting."

"And the Bucks have just reclaimed the lead with fourteen seconds left in the half," the announcer proclaimed against the backdrop of screaming fans.

Jason's curious gaze flicked from the television to Devlin. "You feeling okay, Dad?"

"Yeah, I'm fine." Devlin grabbed the remote and turned off the set. "So what's up?"

Grabbing a throw pillow, his son slouched down into the big easy chair. "I thought we might talk." Then he lapsed into silence.

Devlin waited for Jason to continue and when he didn't, he searched for a logical explanation, something to help his son unload what was bottling up his mind. "Problems in school?"

"No."

"Everything okay with your friends?"

"Yeah."

Jason wasn't a talkative sort of kid. Never had been. In the past, however, his son had never had a problem telling him what was bothering him. Then it occurred to him this might be a matter of a more sensitive nature. "Did you want to talk about girls?"

Jason wrinkled his nose. "Girls?"

He rubbed the back of his neck. Damn, the kid wasn't going to make this easy for him. "I know how it is when you're this age. Guys have certain questions about...well, about the birds and the bees. It's okay, you can ask me about anything."

Jason snorted rudely. "Dad, I don't want to talk about sex."

"You don't?" He let the relief swim through him.

"We already learned all that stuff in school years ago."

Devlin wondered if his oldest son didn't know more on the subject than he'd like him to know. He decided not to ask. "So what's going on?"

His son leaned forward, bracing his elbows on his knees. "How come you and Abby don't sleep together?"

Of all the questions Devlin considered his son might ask, this wasn't the one. In fact, it wasn't even on his list. The query left Devlin floundering for an explanation. "Paige isn't ready to move into her room yet."

Jason's eyes widened and then narrowed. "Paige has been sleeping in her room for almost a week."

Devlin hadn't realized that. Abby had never mentioned it, but then, why should she? "We wanted to make sure Paige was comfortable with her room first."

Jason was watching him closely, and Devlin could tell his son didn't believe his lame answer. Finally Jason said, "There's nothing wrong, is there? She's not much of a cook, but Abby's okay. You're not going to get a divorce or kick her out for some reason, are you?"

"What the hell—"

Before he could vent his anger and tell his son in no uncertain terms what he thought of his suggestion, Jason blurted out, "Dad, Abby needs us."

Devlin's anger left as fast as it had flared. "Why do you think that?"

"She gave up her one and only James Dean picture because she said she has us now."

"And you're afraid she might want the picture back if she leaves?" He didn't like to think his son was that selfish, but he didn't have a clue where this conversation was headed.

Jason scowled at him. "It's just a picture. I mean, to me it's just a picture. But to Abby, that's all she had when she was a kid. At least when Mom left, we still had each other. You, me and Riley. But Abby didn't have anybody when she was my age, she just had a picture of James Dean. Of course, she's got Paige now. But listening to Big Bird and Barbie talk all day gets pretty boring, you know what I mean?"

For a kid of few words, his son suddenly had a lot to say. Devlin settled deeper into the couch. Just to make sure he hadn't misunderstood, he asked his question carefully, "So you want Abby and Paige to stay?"

Jason shrugged and flipped the lever of the recliner so his feet shot straight out. Anchoring his hands behind his head, he pretended to be indifferent. Only the wiggling of his foot gave him away. "It doesn't really matter to me. I'll be out of here in a few years. But I think Riley might need someone to keep an eye on him while you're working."

"You think so?"

"I can't watch over him forever, you know."

"Is that what you thought I expected?"

Jason lifted his shoulders again. "It's not a big deal. He's okay. So is Paige. She sometimes needs a guy around to help tie her shoes and stuff."

"And the baby?"

Jason pretended to study his feet. "I suppose it will cry a lot."

"Sometimes babies do."

A familiar brooding expression descended upon his son's face as he contemplated his shoelaces and tinkered with the loops. "I can always get some new headphones. That might make it easier. Then it wouldn't be so bad."

"Possibly." Devlin averted his eyes so Jason couldn't see the laughter lurking just below the surface. He'd hoped that Jason would come around someday, but he hadn't dared hoped for a breakthrough so soon.

He wondered what Abby had done to trigger the change and make Jason become protective of her. He doubted that had even been her intention, but whatever she'd said to him, it had worked.

Jason didn't linger after that. Apparently, he'd gotten everything off his chest and could retreat with a clear conscience.

Devlin wished he could be as easily placated.

He admired Abby's way of dealing with Jason. She'd coaxed him out of his room to help with the meals, plus she'd broken down the wall of resistance the boy had erected between himself and the family.

Yet, her method of reaching Jason had been to trade a possession she'd kept with her for years. James Dean. She might not have needed the picture, but did that mean she was committed to staying? Or was it just the price she had to pay in order to entice Jason out of his room and into the kitchen?

If only he knew how he could coax Abby to forget about the contract and the money she thought she owed him.

So far, nothing in the terms they'd drawn up had netted him any satisfaction. If anything, he couldn't be more dissatisfied than he already was.

He knew his attraction wasn't one-sided. Abby had responded to the kiss, putting heart and soul into the mating of their lips. But that didn't mean she would easily turn her back on the contract they'd signed.

She'd only had a picture of a movie idol when she was growing up. She'd never known from one year to the next where she would be living and who would be picking her up after school. Her marriage to a man who'd left her with a mountain of debts only cemented the reality of her childhood: never trust anyone.

Devlin knew his chances of breaking down those formidable barriers were slim. But he had to try.

He wanted Abby, body and soul.

He wanted a real wife.

Chapter Eight

By the time Friday arrived—a cool mid-May day despite the full-throttle sunshine—Abby had it all figured out.

After she dropped Paige at preschool, she'd go to the home-decorating store and pick out wallpaper for Paige's room. During the rest of the day, she could paste and apply the paper before getting ready to go to the Castners'. Then on Saturday, she could devote her energies to cleaning out Devlin's office files.

She doubted Devlin had ever cleaned out a scrap of paper. He had his tax returns lumped together with his construction bids, some of them dating back ten years or more. She needed to separate the files, box up whatever wasn't current and store them in the attic. She figured she had at least a full day's work ahead of her, if not more. That was good. She'd need it.

Anything to keep her mind off the fact that she would be home alone with Devlin for the entire weekend.

She dared not remember the last time they were alone,

just the two of them, in an empty house. Yet, all too often during the past week she did remember their wedding night. It was as if every moment was permanently engraved in her mind. The way Devlin's scent stroked and titillated her senses. The strength and excitement of his rough yet tender hands pleasuring her skin. The naked feel of his body stretched against hers.

Dangerous thoughts.

"Mommy." Paige's voice jarred Abby back to the present. "Can Princess come with me to my new grandpa and grandma's house?" She bounced on her bed as she watched Abby pack her purple jogging outfit into the shiny pink suitcase. "Princess has never stayed overnight with them, either."

Her daughter had been talking nonstop about staying at Devlin's parents' ever since she'd gotten up this morning.

"No, I think your grandpa and grandma would prefer that Princess stay here."

Just then, Devlin arrived at Paige's bedroom door. "Need any help?" he asked.

Paige hopped off the bed and skipped to his side. Tucking her small hand inside his, she gave him a dimpled smile that was clearly intended to get her way. "Daddy, can I take Princess with me to Grandma and Grandpa Hamilton's house?"

Devlin hunkered down and tapped her upturned nose. "It's going to be awfully lonely with you three gone. I'm afraid we'll need Princess to stay here and keep us company. Is that okay with you?"

Paige crossed her arms in front of her chest and drew a deep sigh of disappointment. "I suppose so."

He ruffled her hair and stood up again. "Why don't

you go downstairs and see if there are any games you want to bring along?''

Paige screwed up her face. "Who will play them with me? Riley doesn't like to play my games. He says they're dumb."

"Grandpa will. He loves to play games."

"Even my kind of games?"

"Especially your games."

"Oh, goody." Forgetting about her beloved cat, she ran past Devlin and out the door. They could hear her feet clattering down the stairs and into the family room.

"For a little thing, she sure does have heavy feet," Devlin commented as Abby shut the suitcase and snapped the latch.

She started to swing the suitcase off the bed. "At least we always know where she's at."

Devlin reached over and intercepted the small piece of luggage. "I'll put it in the car."

"Now?" She wished he didn't look quite so attractive in a new pair of blue jeans and a plaid shirt with the sleeves rolled halfway to his elbows. He wasn't wearing his usual work clothes, for a change. "I didn't think we were going to drop off the kids until after dinner tonight."

"That was the original plan, but my mother called and asked if they could pick Paige up from preschool and the boys from school. I didn't think there would be a problem, so I agreed." He paused. "There isn't a problem, is there?"

She picked up Paige's pillow and fluffed it. "No. That's fine. I thought I'd work on wallpapering today. That will give me more time to—"

She stopped fluffing at the sight of his shaking head.

"No kids, no work this weekend."

He plucked the pillow from her fingers and tossed it on top of the bedcovers. "This will be our weekend to play. Just you and me."

Before she had a chance to assimilate this change of events, he added, "After we go to your doctor's appointment, that is. It is your monthly appointment today, isn't it?"

Her empty hands automatically curved over her stomach. She was four and a half months along, and since this was her second pregnancy she had started to blossom. "You want to go to my checkup?"

"We both should be there. It's my baby, too." He reached over and propelled her away from the bed and toward him. "Afterward, I figured we could do some fun things."

"Fun things?" She sounded like an idiot, mimicking his words. But Abby didn't know which had her in more of a tailspin, the idea of going to the doctor with Devlin or spending the entire weekend having *fun* with him. Both of them made her heartbeat do a hop, skip and a jump.

So did the mysterious glint in his gaze. What kind of fun did he have in mind?

Before she could ask, Devlin carried the suitcase from the room.

For the next hour, they both kept busy getting the kids off to school and loading the suitcases into the car. By the time they left Paige at her preschool and talked to her teachers about Devlin's parents picking her up later, they had just a few minutes to spare before Abby's appointment.

Entering the doctor's office, Abby noticed that Devlin was the only man in the waiting room. He didn't seem at all uncomfortable to be surrounded by wall-to-wall pregnant women, however. They sat down next to a young woman who had clearly reached the outer limits of her tentlike maternity dress.

"Is this your first one?" Abby asked her.

The woman, who had to be in her early- to mid-twenties, pushed swollen fingers through short brown hair. "I'm already two weeks overdue. I don't know if this baby is so content he doesn't want to move or if he's just plain stubborn."

"Perhaps he's a bit of both."

The woman tried to smile. "It gets kind of long after a while. Is this your first baby, too?"

Devlin, who had slipped his arm around the back of Abby's chair, answered her, "This will be our fourth."

"Fourth?" The woman's voice softened with awe, her hazel gaze flitting between the two and settling on the position of Devlin's arm. "How do you do it? You must give each other lots of support."

Abby smiled. "Parenting is pretty demanding."

The young woman nodded her head. "You two must love each other very much to have that many kids."

She didn't seem to expect an answer as her fingers nervously picked at a seam on her dress. "Ronnie says, all we have to do is love each other more than anyone or anything else in the world and our children will be stable and secure. Children adjust to anything so long as they have parents who love them."

The nurse came around the corner. "Mrs. Armstrong?"

The woman next to them hoisted herself to her feet. "That's me."

"Good luck," Abby said.

"Thanks." She heaved a big sigh. "I'll need it." Then she followed the nurse.

Abby watched her waddle away. "I remember how nervous I was when I was pregnant with Paige. There are so many doubts. So many questions. You wonder how you can possibly be a good parent when you know so little about raising a child," she mused. "I tried to read every book I could. But no situation ever quite matches what the experts say. In the end, all I could do was love her and follow my instincts."

She suddenly realized how close Devlin was sitting to her. He hadn't removed his arm and was studying her with an unnerving intensity. She laughed a bit self-consciously. "Sorry, was I rambling?"

"You don't ramble." Devlin wanted to pull his wife into his arms and kiss her. "Love is all any of us need. It's the ingredient to happiness."

A shadow of wistfulness entered Abby's eyes, hinting at a deeper suppressed emotion. Before he had a chance to analyze it and decode its secrets, Abby quickly lowered her gaze, closing the doorway to her thoughts. What did it mean? Was she starting to have real feelings for him? A bud of hope sprang to life. If there was a chance that Abby was falling in love with him, he was going to do his best to fan any small flame.

The same nurse reappeared. "Mrs. Hamilton?"

Devlin rose and assisted Abby to her feet.

The nurse led them down the short hall and then stopped next to a big scale.

Abby all but groaned aloud as she eyed the ugly, lying monster in front of her. That machine always made her ten pounds heavier than she was, and there was nothing more humiliating to a woman than to be weighed in front of a man.

Through the veil of her lashes, she eyed Devlin. "I

don't suppose you'd be willing to disappear for thirty seconds."

Devlin, bless his obstinate soul, dared to look at her with a feigned innocence even a baby wouldn't believe. "Don't mind me. We're in this together, remember?"

"Then you step on the scale."

His glaze glittered. "You want me to hold your hand?"

Odious man. She wouldn't give him the satisfaction of letting him believe his opinion mattered. Without looking at him, she hiked up on the scale, refusing to flinch when the nurse read aloud, "One hundred and twenty-six pounds. You're doing just fine."

Ignoring Devlin's extended hand, Abby stepped off the scale as if it were a simmering bed of hot coals. When she brushed by him, Devlin said in a low voice that only she could hear, "I'll still love you even when you weigh a hundred and sixty-six."

The word *love* made her heartbeat race to her throat. She knew he didn't mean it. She tried to cover her reaction by shooting him a withering look.

After the nurse showed them into the examination room, they barely had time to sit down when the doctor, a short Oriental man with a friendly smile, came in. "Good morning, Mrs. Hamilton."

"Dr. Lee, this is my husband, Devlin."

The doctor reached over and shook Devlin's hand. "It's nice to have you here. We like to encourage both parents to attend the appointments and the Lamaze classes." He picked up the chart. "You have signed up for the classes, correct?"

"Not yet," Abby said. She had considered it but hadn't wanted to put Devlin on the spot and make him feel pressured into attending.

Devlin's eyebrow lifted in a quizzical manner. "Have they already started?"

The doctor pulled a calendar from the pocket of his white coat and flipped it open. "There's a new class starting next week. You can sign up at the reception desk before you leave, if you'd like."

Much to Abby's surprise, Devlin didn't hesitate. "Consider it done."

Dr. Lee tucked away his calendar and patted the examining table. "Okay, Abby, let's take a look and see how things are coming along."

Fortunately, the examination was fairly impersonal, even though her protruding stomach was exposed. Devlin stayed seated while the doctor did his job, and that made it easier for Abby to relax and respond to the doctor's directions and comments.

Finally, the doctor turned toward Devlin. "Would you like to hear your son or daughter's heartbeat?"

Devlin moved to Abby's side and put on the earpiece. She barely breathed as she peered through her lashes and watched a surge of emotion flow across Devlin's face. His gaze met hers. Mirrored in the bottomless pools of green, she saw incredulity mix with wonderment.

Emotions from deep inside of her welled and overflowed.

When Devlin had announced he would be coming with her today, it had seemed wiser and safer not to attach any meaning or expectation to his decision. For all she knew, he would plant himself in the waiting room, as her first husband had done, while she visited the doctor. John hadn't ever been comfortable with the physical evidence of her pregnancy.

But with Devlin, there was no hesitation. No revulsion. One of his hands clasped hers while his other hand gently—and almost reverently—caressed the mound of her stomach. She wanted to weep from the pure beauty of it all. It was all she could do not to raise up on her elbows and kiss him for this priceless moment of joy and sharing.

Later that night, Abby had trouble keeping her attention trained on the CLUE game board in front of her.

Part of the reason for her distraction rested on the fascinating Castners.

As soon as Cash took their coats, Abby had been struck by the energy and harmony intermingling through the house.

They'd given her the grand tour of their home. The three-thousand-foot three-story had been built by Devlin's company. Each room had a distinct personality. Cash had decorated half the rooms and Rebecca the other because they hadn't been able to agree on the decor.

Rebecca preferred Victorian antiques, her set of rooms containing special treasures that she'd acquired through the years.

Cash's rooms, on the other hand, favored, in his wife's words, "carnival riffraff."

Cash's living room boasted Rolling Stones memorabilia and a Zsa Zsa Gabor picture on one side. In the far corner, a stuffed pig with silver wings sat next to a Cat Woman cutout. Probably the most prominent feature belonged to the Green Bay Packers' cheesehead, mounted in a place of honor above the gray-stoned fireplace. The cheesehead had become a recognizable state symbol, and Abby could easily picture Cash wearing the yellow triangular piece of foam, shaped like a wedge of cheese, at a Packers' football game along with the other zealot Packer fans.

The room should have looked cheap and gaudy. In actuality it was oddly charming…as charming as Cash and Rebecca, who had bickered nonstop from the moment Mrs. White landed in the conservatory in search of the knife.

"If you don't stop trying to peek at my cards, you're going to sleep in the cellar with all the other rats," Rebecca snapped at her husband, cradling her cards protectively against her bosom.

"I already know that you have Colonel Mustard, the lead pipe and the dining room." Cash's smugness was accompanied by a long, smooth drawl designed to provoke his wife. "I'm just curious which card you showed Devlin."

She treated him to a disdainful glare. "Give it up, Cash. You used that bluff two games ago. I didn't buy it then and I'm not buying it now."

"Are you saying I'm a liar, too?" her husband asked.

"Keep your hands above the table where I can see them."

"Sorry, was that your knee I squeezed, honey?" Cash's wide-eyed expression was foiled by a ruthless grin.

"It had better be." Devlin angled his cards away from his good buddy's viewing range. "I don't take kindly to you pawing my wife, old man."

Cash leaned toward Abby who was seated on his right. "Ouch, can you believe how vicious those two are? They get plain mean when they don't win."

Abby couldn't restrain a smile. "It's amazing how well you're holding up."

"I've figured out a secret for surviving."

Her mouth quirked. "You have?"

"Yep." He waggled his eyebrows. "I make it into foreplay."

Even though he spoke in a whisper directed toward her ear, he spoke loud enough for both Devlin and Rebecca to hear.

"Cash—" Rebecca's voice dripped with warning "—do you have the rope, Miss Scarlet or the ballroom?"

Cash winked at Abby. "See what I mean? Miss Scarlet in the ballroom with a rope? The possibilities are endless."

"Cash, are you playing this game or talking Abby's ear off?" Rebecca's exasperation didn't contain an ounce of anger.

In the back of Rebecca's eyes, Abby could see the sliver of laughter and wished the evening could go on forever. Especially since the Castners' byplay made it easier to keep her attention locked on them and not on the man who was seated directly across from her.

She could almost forget that when they left here tonight, she and Devlin would be going home to an empty house. To temptation.

Her hand moved over her stomach and absently rubbed the babe nestled deep inside.

"Abby? It's your turn."

Rebecca's voice brought Abby back to the present. The other three players were watching her curiously. "Sorry, I was daydreaming."

"Good, then maybe I'll have a better shot at winning." Cash winked at her.

"In your dreams, Castner," his wife rebuked him.

Abby made an effort to keep her mind on the game for the rest of the evening.

After the culmination of several games of CLUE, Cash

and Devlin cleared the table while Abby joined Rebecca in the kitchen.

"How's it going with the boys? Have you found it difficult to be a stepmother?" Rebecca asked.

"We have our good days and our average days."

"Sounds about right. What do they think about the baby coming?"

Abby considered the question before answering, "They're not sure what to think. A baby in the house will be an adjustment."

Rebecca nodded. "For us, too."

It took a moment for Rebecca's words to sink in. Abby nearly dropped the napkins. "You're expecting?"

"December. Just a couple of months after you." The happiness in her voice bubbled over. "I was so jealous when I first heard you and Devlin were going to have a baby. We've been trying for almost a year." Rebecca pulled four mugs from the maple cabinets. "I was starting to get worried that something was wrong."

"But there wasn't."

"No. Thank goodness. The doctor kept trying to tell me to relax and let nature take its course. Cash was wonderful. He wouldn't let me get all tangled in a knot. I have a tendency to get uptight when the world isn't rotating on a smooth axis. Cash keeps me grounded when I'm not threatening to hang him up by his bootstraps, that is. I don't know what I would do without him."

A twinge of yearning plucked Abby's heartstrings. She wouldn't let herself be jealous of Rebecca's contentment and excitement. After all, she had so much to be grateful for. "Is Kelly excited?"

Rebecca giggled. "We told her tonight. She wanted to call Paige right away and tell her. I imagine they'll be playing babies from now until we deliver."

"They have a lot of fun together."

"Yes, they do." After she set the mugs on the table, Rebecca touched Abby's arm. "I'm delighted Devlin married you. You've made him very happy and he deserves that happiness."

Abby had to fight back a wave of emotion. "Thank you. You and Cash have been very kind."

Rebecca's expression became shrewd. "You're easy to be kind to, Abby. It's not hard to see why Devlin married you as soon as you met. You're genuine. Do you know this is the first time Devlin's brought a woman to our house since Linda left?"

Abby tried not to read too much into Rebecca's admission. After all, she could understand why Devlin hadn't dated much. "It's tough for a single parent to socialize when you're busy working and trying to raise a family on your own."

Rebecca nodded. "Kids are a challenge even on a good day." She handed Abby the napkins and forks. "I really like your maternity top. Did you get it around here?"

Abby fingered the crisp fabric. "Devlin brought it home from Madison a couple of weeks ago."

Rebecca groaned. "You are so lucky. Cash has absolutely no taste in clothes."

"Says who?" Cash entered the room.

Devlin followed him in. "Don't worry about it, old man, you have wonderful taste in women." Walking over to Rebecca, Devlin gave her a hug and kissed her on the cheek. "What's this I hear about you being a mama again?"

She beamed, laughing up into his face. "We didn't want you to get too far ahead of us. You have to promise me you'll lend Cash your expertise about shopping for women's clothes.''

"I don't do miracles.'' Then he chuckled as he dodged a poke from Cash.

By the time they bundled up in their coats an hour later, Abby was exhausted. Although the conversation was free-flowing, there was an undercurrent of tension growing between her and Devlin.

The big lonely house and separate beds awaited them.

"No kids for the entire weekend? Don't do anything I wouldn't do,'' was Cash's admonition before Devlin claimed Abby's arm to escort her down the steps and into the night.

They wouldn't. They couldn't, Abby thought as she shivered in the cold night air.

A black-and-white contract stood front and center between them.

Why did she suddenly feel so depressed?

Abby was too tired to worry about her depression. As soon as they arrived home, she headed straight for bed. The last thing she remembered hearing before sleep dragged her into slumberland was the sound of the Hide-A-Bed being pulled across the floor.

Early the next morning, Abby's eyes popped open as a large dry tongue licked her lips.

"Dammit, Hulk, get down.'' Devlin's face came into focus. A bit blurry around the edges at first, then more detailed. He looked both determined and frustrated.

Abby blinked, attempting to remove the sleep from her eyes and figure out what was going on. She got one more glimpse of Devlin before the dog lunged at her again and she was *French-kissed* by the exuberant canine. "Ugh!''

"That does it! You're out of here,'' Devlin growled.

He plunked down the tray he had in his hands on top of the dresser before dragging the protesting mutt out the door.

Within seconds he returned to pick up the tray and set it across her lap.

Shifting gingerly, she grappled with the strap of her nightgown that had slipped off the edge of her right shoulder and exposed the swell of one breast. "You didn't have to make me breakfast." Under Devlin's brooding gaze, she felt practically naked.

As if it had a mind of its own, the strap dropped over the side again.

Before she could retrieve it, Devlin reached and slid it up again, his blunt-edged fingers leaving a trail of goose-flesh in their wake. "You're not the only one who can make eggs," he said.

His husky baritone did strange things to her nerves. She almost sank beneath the blanket, wanting to pull the blankets up around her ears. It was hard enough to wake up to a dog kissing her. It was even harder to wake up to the reality of having Devlin in the bedroom with her. Pulling herself together as best she could, she picked up the fork. "Are you going to join me?"

"I only had one tray. I figured we could share if you don't mind."

She offered him the other fork. "Help yourself."

He sat down on the edge of the bed and dug in.

Abby couldn't raise an appetite for toast, eggs and juice. Not with Devlin sitting so deliciously close. The sun winked through the shuttered windows, casting the bedroom in a warm intimacy.

The only thing she could see was Devlin. His tan-tone flannel shirt, open at the throat, revealed a smooth, tanned neck and complemented his sea-green eyes. Faded jeans showcased his long legs and lean hips to perfection. Because it was Saturday, he'd forsaken his work boots and wore soft-sided moccasins.

Everything about him oozed male.

Everything inside of her responded female.

She wiggled.

Devlin paused from taking another bite. "Your back bothering you?"

"Just a bit."

He grabbed a pillow from the other side of the bed and gave it a few punches before leaning over and stuffing it carefully behind her. "Better?" he asked.

She nodded, her mouth too dry to form the words. Her back did feel better but having him monitoring her movements hadn't soothed her jittery pulse rate. If anything, she was more aware of him than ever. She seemed fixated on every ripple his body made. From the motion of his Adam's apple to the flex of his hands as he maneuvered his fork.

She rested her fork.

"The eggs don't set well?" he asked.

"No. They taste fine. Everything does. I guess I'm still full from last night."

He nodded. "Rebecca loves to cook and she was anxious to impress you."

"You've been friends a long time, haven't you?"

"Almost all my life. Cash and Rebecca started going together in the fifth grade."

"Fifth grade?" She leaned back into the pillows and just decided to enjoy watching him eat. The simple pleasure filled her with an odd contentment. "In this day and age, it's hard to imagine a relationship withstanding all those teenage years and then evolving into a strong marriage."

Devlin finally put down his napkin and pulled the tray from the bed. Then he relaxed on his forearms. "They've had their ups and downs. For a long time, they didn't think Rebecca could have children. And when she got pregnant, she ended up spending the last three months in bed so she wouldn't lose Kelly. Cash was beside himself with worry."

A network of pained lines spiraling from the corners of his eyes caused Abby's heart to squeeze in commiseration. The bond he shared with his friends had a history of deep love. "They love each other very much, don't they?"

"Yes, they do. No matter what has happened, they've always had each other."

"I guess that's real love. The kind they write about in fairy tales." Her words sounded almost whimsical, with a hint of longing she couldn't mask.

He turned on his side and faced her. The intensity radiating from him was almost palpable. Every tendon in his neck stood at attention, clearly defined as if he was trying to hold back something. She swallowed. Was he wishing for the love that his friends had? Was he regretting that he'd settled for half a package instead of waiting until love had come along?

A large ball of need built up inside of her. Her fingers clutched the bedsheets and her naughty nightgown strap took a nosedive down her arm again.

Devlin's gaze zeroed in on hers. She couldn't look away. She saw a hunger there. Burning. Raw. Uncensored. The quiet in the room writhed and simmered, taking on a turbulent life of its own. Time stretched to a snapping point. She wished she could decipher the cryptic message. He wanted something from her. But she didn't know what. Had he had an ulterior motive for fixing her breakfast?

Finally, he broke the silence between them. "What would you like to do today?"

She grabbed her shoulder strap and thrust it back into place. Trying to be as nonchalant as possible, she reached for the bed covers and attempted to cover herself. "If you have work to do, don't feel you have to entertain me. With the kids at your parents', I can always sit back and enjoy a book."

He frowned. "I thought we might do something together."

She tried to relax her death hold on the sheets. "What did you have in mind?" Then she caught sight of him rubbing the base of his neck. "Your back is sore?"

He grimaced. "I slept in the wrong position."

Attempting to sound as nonchalant as possible, she said, "Why don't you sleep in here since this is the bigger bed, and I'll take the Hide-A-Bed?"

"No." His flat pronouncement didn't leave room for argument.

She hadn't expected anything different. Her husband had a strong sense of right and wrong. But she was equally as determined. "It's only fair that I take my turn. You should be getting a good night's sleep."

He shook his head. "You're not sleeping on that Hide-A-Bed. As the baby grows and moves, you'll need a good mattress with lots of support."

"Then we'll share this bed. There's plenty of room for both of us." By not so much as a tremor did she reveal her own uncertainty at suggesting such a solution. She knew Devlin didn't want to sleep with her. He'd made that abundantly clear by not moving into the room with her after Paige had finally taken the big step to sleep in her own room. However, he couldn't continue to sleep on that awful couch. It was more than evident he was paying a price for the sleepless nights.

A tic disturbed the set to his jaw. "I don't think I can do that."

She refused to flinch. He wasn't trying to hurt her. She knew that. But the stab to her midsection was deep. "I'll try not to toss and turn too much."

Without warning, he moved. His arm came down around her, snagging her close to his side. His leg covered hers, trapping and holding her still. "I don't care if you thrash in your sleep. Or snore. Or sing."

"Then what is it?" There was no way to brace herself for his answer. Not when she was in such a vulnerable position.

"I'm a man, not a vegetable," The terseness in his voice echoed the tension in his face. "I can't sleep in the same bed with you and not make love to you."

Chapter Nine

It was as if a giant whirlwind sucked all the air from Abby's lungs. Staring up into Devlin's face, she saw the tight rein he held on his emotions. His arm hugged her closer to the heat of his body. "That's why you haven't moved into the bedroom?" she whispered, hardly daring to hope in case she'd misunterstood.

He nodded.

"Why didn't you tell me?"

He picked up her hand and put it to his mouth. Turning it just so, he kissed the inside of her palm and then the sensitive pulse inside her wrist. "This wasn't part of our agreement. But I want you so bad it hurts. I can't stop thinking about how wonderful we were together." The hardness of his body against hers reiterated his words.

Abby froze. On the tip of her tongue were the words *I want you, too.* But something kept them locked inside.

Suddenly, Devlin pulled himself off the bed and stood on the floor. "Why don't you get dressed and we can drive to Madison for the day?'' His voice wasn't quite steady despite the impersonal tone.

A chill dashed along her exposed skin. She instantly missed the heat and protectiveness of his body. "Don't you want to discuss this?"

"There's nothing to discuss. This is my problem, not yours." He picked up the tray, turned away and walked toward the door. "While you're getting ready, I'll take care of these dishes. I'll meet you downstairs."

He left behind a void of emptiness. Abby's head spun with questions and impossible answers. Devlin wanted her. That knowledge both scared and thrilled her.

She wanted him, too. And that scared her more than she thought possible. The temptation to call him back almost overcame her common sense. If Devlin hadn't shut the door, she might have heeded the desire. As it was, the matter was decided for her.

Pushing aside her confusion and wanton fantasies, she slipped out of bed, grabbed her robe and headed toward the shower.

Twenty minutes later, she finished drying her hair, using her fingers to shape the carefree layers. Conscious of Devlin waiting for her downstairs, she kept her mind firmly channeled on the job at hand. Giving her thoughts permission to wander wouldn't accomplish anything right now.

It was safer not to think.

For today, she would let nature take its course. They had the entire day together. She didn't want a single moment to be strained and uncomfortable. They'd both had enough of that. Even though it was clear they both wanted something more from their relationship, they weren't ready to confront the next step.

They needed a few lighthearted hours together.

If that was possible.

Wearing a new blue-denim maternity jumper that Devlin's sister, Gayle, had sent her, Abby arrived in the kitchen as Devlin was hanging up the phone.

She felt ridiculously pleased at the glint of approval in his gaze. He snagged the keys from the wooden hook near the door. "Ready to go?"

"Where to?"

"With the baby coming, we might want to go shopping for a baby crib and some extra furniture. After that, we can see how you feel and plan our day accordingly." He reached into the closet and pulled out their coats. "Does that sound okay to you?"

It wasn't what her heart longed to do, but his plan sounded safe and practical. She pushed her arms into the sleeves. "Lead the way."

The grin he flashed her didn't do a thing for her blood pressure. "I love a woman who will follow her man anywhere."

If only that were true, she thought as she passed in front of him while he held open the door.

Devlin had hoped this trip to town might ease some of the tension between them. He knew they couldn't spend the weekend in the house, just the two of them, without him either going stark raving mad or tumbling Abby into bed.

They needed some time together where they could be at ease, even though he feared he was facing an uphill battle. The truth was, the more he was around Abby, the more he wanted to be with her. Emotionally and physically. He needed her.

At the third store, Abby fell head over heels in love with a beautiful canopy-covered crib.

"Like it?" Devlin had seen the soft wistful expression take over his wife's face. There was a yearning quality he couldn't resist.

She ran her fingertips lovingly across the carved oak railing. "It's exquisite."

"There's a dresser and changing table to match."

She turned and walked over to the dressing table. "When I was a little girl, I dreamed about things like this. It was part of my dream list."

"Dream list?"

She reddened a bit. "It was a list that I made in my head of all the things I would buy when I grew up and had my own home." She shook her head and laughed. "Of course, life doesn't always accommodate wishes. When I got pregnant with Paige, we didn't have enough money, and we borrowed a neighbor's crib."

Determination flooded through Devlin. If any woman deserved to have her fantasies fulfilled, it was Abby. She was the most giving woman he'd ever met.

Beckoning to the saleswoman who had been standing a discreet distance away, giving them space and time to examine the merchandise, he pointed to the crib grouping. "Do you have this furniture in stock?"

The dark-haired woman peered at the tag, which was attached to the side of the crib. "Let me check. I'll be right back."

After the sales clerk hurried away, Abby said in a low voice that couldn't be overheard by anyone else, "I didn't mean we had to buy this crib set. It's awfully expensive."

Devlin stared into her big blue eyes that were wide

with doubt. "The baby needs a crib and this is the one you like, correct?"

"But the baby will only be able to use it for a few years. What will we do with it then?"

It was on the tip of his tongue to suggest they could have six more kids if it would make her stay with him. Trapping her wasn't what he wanted. He wanted Abby to stay with him because she *wanted* to.

Because she loved him.

Just as he loved her.

The realization hit him with the force of a sledgehammer. Under the fluorescent lights, the floor seemed to shift beneath his feet as he gripped the edge of the crib. Hell, why hadn't he realized it before?

He loved her.

He should have recognized it. Perhaps on some gut level he'd always known.

How long he'd loved her, he wasn't sure. It seemed as if his feelings for her had been a part of him forever.

Maybe when he'd first seen her at his sister's house on the night of the anniversary party. He'd certainly felt something for her then.

Admiration for her gutsiness to try to fix the roof.

Fascination with the way she kept a house and still managed to tend to her daughter's needs.

Appreciation for the way she looked in the formfitting jumpsuit she'd worn.

One desire on top of another had snowballed into a need to be with her. A need to marry her and tie her to him forever. He'd come up with the contract idea as the fastest and shortest way to make her his wife.

Now that she was, he wondered at his idiocy. He should have done it right. He should have courted her as Abby deserved to be courted. She'd been deprived of a childhood. Her marriage had been nothing less than a charade. He should have seen that she needed more.

But he, too, had shortchanged her. Of all the things he'd done in his life, he'd jeopardized her greatest chance for happiness. And his?

Was it too late?

Why should Abby believe his sincerity now?

Could she ever let go of the past and love him without that damn contract hanging like a noose around his neck?

Abby's hand covered the rigid muscles in his arm. "Devlin, are you okay?"

"Sorry, I guess I must not have gotten enough sleep last night." As he struggled to regroup, he could see Abby wasn't convinced by his glib explanation. But now wasn't the time to plead his case and undo all the mistakes he'd made.

He pulled the checkbook from his back pocket. "Let's order this bedroom set and then after the baby has outgrown it, we'll save it for our grandchildren."

Abby didn't seem convinced, chewing on the side of her lip as she was apt to do when she was thinking. "Maybe I should help pay for—"

"It's our money. Everything I own is yours."

Did she understand what he was trying to say?

He wanted a future with her where they shared and shared alike. He understood that she'd always had to pay her own way. But that was with people who had never really loved her.

Not the way he did, with that heart-thudding certainty that this was the woman he wanted in his life and bed forever.

But Abby had heard promises like that all her life. They'd been broken time and time again. She'd learned to be cautious. Learned to trust in half measures.

It couldn't be like that between them. He had to make her fall in love with him, keep her a bit off balance so she couldn't put her past between them.

He had to seduce her in such a way that she'd willingly tear up the contract between them.

After they arranged to have the crib set delivered, Devlin took her to a nice Chinese restaurant for lunch. "Do you want to shop some more or tour the Parade of Homes?" he asked after they were finished eating.

"I've met my quota of shopping for one day," Abby said. "What is the Parade of Homes?"

The Parade of Homes, she learned, was an annual event that showcased thirty or so brand-new homes. Most of them had been presold and were located in four different areas in the greater Madison area.

As Devlin swung the car through the streets in a community outside of Madison, he pointed out several new businesses along Main Street. "This used to be a small community that centered around farming. But during the past few years, people from Madison have started moving eastward."

"Have you built any homes around here?"

He shook his head. "I've built several north of here in Sun Prairie."

While Abby could appreciate the decors and structures in the different houses they visited, what she enjoyed the most was listening to and learning about Devlin—the contractor and the businessman—as they strolled through the elegantly attired homes.

The first house they visited was beautifully situated on a large lot at the end of a cul-de-sac, an ideal location with a number of mature oak trees shading the property.

Abby loved the deck that wrapped around three sides of the house and looked over the picturesque setting.

As they walked through the handsomely decorated two-story house, Devlin examined some new gadgetry while Abby explored the kitchen. The center island in the middle of the room was large enough for six people to sit around, and she could easily imagine a family sitting there for snacks or breakfast.

The rest of the house was equally impressive, with three roomy bedrooms, two fireplaces and hardwood floors throughout.

But as charming as the house was, Abby found her attention centered on Devlin. Despite her lack of knowledge of building materials and the industry in general, he'd ask her opinion about a particular feature. Furthermore, he had a habit of taking her hand as they'd walk from room to room, reconfirming the intimacy that had blossomed the day before in the doctor's office.

The awareness between them manifested itself. Feeding on each time he touched her. Each time he listened. He made her feel important and special. That was both comforting and threatening.

Abby knew she should be worried about the dangers of letting down her guard, but she couldn't seem to resurrect her old barriers. Not with the unforgettable knowledge that Devlin wanted her.

Wanted *her*, Abigail O'Reilly Hamilton. Pregnant and a debt hanging over her head, and he still wanted her.

She couldn't forget his confession. She didn't want to. The reality was equally scary and intriguing.

The fourth house they visited became her favorite. She loved everything, from the stone-brick fireplace in the family room to the large master bedroom that took up half the second floor. But it was the bathroom that captivated her soul.

When they walked into the sumptuous bathroom, she stopped short. A large whirlpool bath, big enough for two people, sat in the middle of the chic interior. Shiny black cabinets, a big marble counter and reflective mirrors on all four walls made the room rich and inviting. A groan escaped Abby's lips. "This is either heaven or belongs in a rich man's harem."

"Like it?" Devlin leaned against the doorway, looking relaxed except for his watchful eyes.

She ran her fingers across the marble vanity. "I could live in that whirlpool bath forever. It's decadent, extravagant and perfect. Real people don't have bathrooms like this, do they?"

"You would be surprised how many real people do. In particular, women love these bathrooms." He slowly dimmed the lights. Shimmering sensuality shrouded the room. "Now what do you think?" His voice had dropped to a seductive level.

Smoothing the gooseflesh that sprang up over her arms, she didn't dare tell him what she really thought. Her fantasies were decidedly erotic and R-rated, with Devlin playing the lead role.

In the sensual setting, she could easily imagine them sharing the tub-for-two, picturing Devlin's naked shoulders rising about the frothy water, feeling the sleekness of his skin against hers. In her mind's eye, he would lean over her and place his lips to her throat, blazing a trail of kisses along her pulse points.

"Abby?"

At the sound of her name, Abby jerked back to reality. She saw Devlin straighten and take a step toward her.

She held out a hand to ward him off. It was hard

enough to think when he was standing six feet away. If he moved any closer, she didn't know what she'd do. "I'm fine. Really. I've never seen a room like this before." She knew her words were tumbling over each other without rhyme or reason.

The prudent thing to do was escape before she did something that would embarrass them both. "I don't think a room like this is what we need for the baby."

His gaze stroked hers. "No, this isn't for a baby or the kids. It's strictly for adults." Devlin quit moving toward her but continued to watch her closely, the intensity cranking up a notch. "For us. I think it would be a good idea for us to add a bathroom similar to this to the house. We could use it at the end of a long day when all the kids are in bed. Doesn't that sound relaxing?"

Sharing a hot tub with Devlin would be anything but relaxing. Stimulating. Hot. Seductive. Yes. But relaxing? Not until her sex drive shriveled up from disuse. Even then, she doubted being with Devlin in a sea of bubbles would be relaxing. "Something like this costs a lot of money."

"Money isn't an object."

For him, it probably never had been. She searched for another possible excuse to keep him from building temptation onto the house. "When would you have time to build it? Summer is your busy time."

"My crew needs one more project to fill in this summer. No reason they can't build a bathroom and extra bedroom for us."

He had an answer for everything. Or so it seemed. She wished she had the courage to ask him what he was really proposing. But she didn't. "Why didn't you add a room like this when you built the house?"

"I didn't see a purpose or have a need for it."

And he did now?

Even though he hadn't moved, she felt surrounded by him.

He wants you.

But for how long? What would happen when he got tired of her? When the newness between them waned?

They couldn't stay locked up in a bathroom forever.

Desire couldn't be sustained. Then what would happen?

"We'd turn into prunes." She'd said the first thing that came to her mind.

Devlin's gaze claimed hers. "I'll rub lotion on your back if you rub some on mine."

Oh, Lord. Was he trying to drive her crazy?

Her husband stood with his feet apart and his thumbs anchored on the edges of his jean pockets, bold desire gleaming from his gaze. The man didn't play fair.

Desperate, she shut her eyes against the steamy images he provoked and implanted on her senses. For both their sakes, she needed to put an end to this. They'd only regret it later if they let things get out of hand now. Using the only defense weapon she had left, she forced a yawn.

Fortunately, she didn't have to feign one. After being on her feet most of the day, she was tired. And given the amount of energy she'd had to raise to combat her emotions, she was dog-tired.

Suddenly, the full wattage of light returned. She blinked at Devlin.

Concern had chased away the high voltage of passion on his face. "You look like you need a nap. Are you ready to go?"

She nodded. But she couldn't resist taking one more lingering look at the bathroom.

As he took her arm, Devlin said, "I've got the manufacturer's brochure and several others. We can look at them later if you like.''

Liking was not the problem.

Abby slept most of the way home. When they walked into the house, Devlin steered her to the bedroom. He pushed her gently down on the bed and pulled off her shoes. She couldn't raise her eyelids or open her mouth to thank him when he drew the bedcovers over her and then quietly left the room.

Waking several hours later, she checked the digital clock sitting on top of the dresser and saw it was nearly seven o'clock. She couldn't believe she'd slept so long. Pushing back the blankets, she swung her feet off the bed and was halfway across the floor when the door opened and Devlin came in.

"Sleep okay?"

"I think I slumbered with the dead."

He grinned at her. "Welcome back to the living. Are you hungry?"

"Starved."

"You want to go out to eat or rustle up something here?"

It would probably be smarter to get dressed and go out to eat, but she didn't have the desire to be smart right now. The kids would be returning in the morning and they wouldn't get too many opportunities to eat at home, just the two of them. Alone. "Let's eat here."

It didn't take them long to prepare a quick but satisfying meal. They talked about the kids, Devlin's construction jobs for the summer and other safe subjects.

As they adjourned to the kitchen to do the dishes together, Devlin insisted on washing.

"You missed a speck of food on this plate," she told him, offering him the dish.

He arched his eyebrow. "Sure you don't want that piece later for a snack?"

"That's mighty considerate of you but I think I'll pass."

"I'm a considerate type of man."

"Humble, too."

"I didn't think you'd noticed."

She'd noticed, all right.

She noticed even more things when his arm brushed against hers as he leaned over to wipe the counter, triggering curlicues of heat inside of her. How had she ever thought she could resist this man?

Did she want to?

After the last dish was put away in the cupboard, Devlin asked, "Want to play a game, watch some television or look at those brochures we brought home?"

A game sounded relatively safe. "What kind of game?"

"Poker?"

She wrinkled her nose. "Do you have Scrabble?"

He groaned. "That's a woman's game."

"I happen to be a woman, in case you haven't noticed."

"Oh, I noticed, all right." His heavy look of desire didn't need an interpreter. "I could teach you the fine points of strip poker."

"I didn't think strip poker had any finer points."

"It depends on what side of the table you're sitting on."

The devil lurked at the back of his green eyes and Abby knew better than to trust him. Why had she thought playing a game would be safe? For some reason, he was trying to stoke the fires raging between them. She decided to take the upper hand. "What other games do you have?"

Devlin didn't seem quite ready to give up his suggestion. "We could get naked right away and then you wouldn't have to worry about losing your clothes."

She refused to be provoked. "I suppose we could each play our own game of Solitaire."

He grimaced, and pulled out a chair from the dining-room table for her to sit in. "I'll check the boys' rooms and see what they've got that still has all the pieces."

He came back with Boggle, a game that Abby had always found stimulating.

But the stimulation she'd enjoyed in the past became a distant memory to the kind Devlin introduced during the game.

After the sand ran through the timer, he read his list aloud. "Big, beg, beged—"

"*Beged* isn't a word," she protested.

"Sure it is."

"No, *begged* is spelled with two *g*'s."

"Not in my dictionary."

She narrowed her gaze. "And what dictionary would that be?"

His leg bumped against hers beneath the table. "The Unabridged You-Don't-Need-Two-*G*'s Dictionary."

"Really?" She tried to move her knee away from his. "I've never seen that dictionary on any bookstore or library shelf."

He flashed her a grin that wouldn't have been admitted in public places as his hand came across the table and cupped hers. "You won't find it any of those places."

"So where would I find it?" She could barely corral her thoughts as his thumb stroked hers.

"On the inside door of the men's rest room at Bart's Gas Station."

She refused to give him the satisfaction of pulling away and letting him believe he'd gotten the best of her. She lifted her chin to a disbelieving angle. "I haven't been in the men's rest room at Bart's Gas Station."

"That's too bad." His sincerity didn't make the grade. "I guess you'll have to take my word for it."

She shook her head. "On the women's side of Bart's Gas Station, they spell it *b-e-g-g-e-d*. And since this is a woman's game, as you put it, we'll have to go by the rules on the female side of the wall."

Lazy amusement gleamed at her. "Are you sure that's on the rest-room walls?"

"Just as sure as you are that *beged* is on the men's side." Her smile would have made a feline proud.

He gave in. Temporarily.

As they played several more games, Devlin defended *bas, pikul* and *loks*.

More than once she threatened to get a real dictionary, but he wouldn't consider it. As their debates heated up, so did the sexual tension between them. Somehow, her legs became trapped inside of his. She couldn't move without generating more friction between them.

The game had become one of sexual undercurrents.

She didn't want the evening to end, for them to go to their separate beds. For tomorrow to come. For the real world to descend and end this chemistry between them.

The clock struck eleven as they finished another game, and Abby looked up to see Devlin watching her. "Ready to call it quits?"

Was his voice huskier and deeper than usual? With the blood pounding in her ears, she couldn't be certain. She licked her lips. "My eyes are starting to see double."

His gaze tracked the movement of her tongue. "Likewise."

She groped for the game box. "We'll have to play it again sometime."

He stood up and looked down at her from his full height. "Next time, I get to choose the game."

After he left to return the game to the bedroom, she got to her feet and walked into the living room. She was too keyed up to sleep. Her legs were a bit stiff from all the sitting, so she walked over to the window and stared out into the night. A cloud had passed over the moon and she could barely make out the craggy face.

A few minutes later, she felt Devlin's presence behind her, the full weight of his gaze upon her.

"I used to talk to the moon when I was a little girl and we'd keep each other company." She rubbed her hands over her arms and turned toward him.

He didn't mock her or ask her why she needed to talk to the moon. "Do you talk to him now?"

"No, I'm not a lonely little girl now."

"Why not?"

"I have a family and everything I've ever wanted."

"Everything?" His question was low and strained. "Do you have everything you really want? Everything you need?"

The silence ticked between them as Abby tried to read his expression. Then she realized that she didn't need to look any deeper than what was on his face. He hadn't made any secret of what he wanted. He was waiting for her to decide what she wanted.

And if she would dare reach for it.

She shook her head. "No, I don't have everything I want."

"Tell me," he demanded, without taking a step closer to her.

He was giving her room to make her own choices, even though the tendons in his neck protruded, underlining the control he was exerting over his own desires.

Outside, thunder suddenly rumbled, just before a streak of lightning sliced open the skies. A few drops of rain hit the roof. Hesitant. A ping here. A pang there.

"It sounds like it's going to rain."

"Is it?" Impatience darkened his tone.

"Yes."

"Say it, Abby. I need to hear the words."

She searched his face for answers to the uncertainty that made her hesitate. Her eyes burned from the need to blink. But she couldn't look away. "This morning you said you couldn't sleep in the same bed with me and not make love to me? Did you mean it?"

"Yes."

The hoarse honesty of his response pulled at her. She couldn't walk away from that kind of need. Even if she wanted to. And she didn't want to. She wanted Devlin. "I don't think I could sleep in the same bed with you, either."

"Don't just tell me what you think I want to hear."

She went to him without hesitation. "I want you, too. I tried not to. I wanted to keep my end of the contract. I—"

He cut her off by pulling her into his arms. "To hell with the bloody contract."

His mouth came down on hers as the skies opened up and dropped pounding rain to the starving earth.

Chapter Ten

Devlin needed Abby more than he'd ever thought it humanly possible to need anyone. His hunger for her was so consuming he didn't know if he could make it to the bedroom.

But he pushed his own desires aside as he carried Abby into the bedroom and placed her gently on the big comforter and then lay down next to her. The intoxicating passion in her eyes nearly made him forget his decision to go slow, to make this right for her.

If ever a woman needed to be loved, it was Abby. She'd learned not to ask for love because such expectations led to inevitable hurt.

Devlin knew he couldn't make up for her past, but he could give her a future and make sure she never went hungry again.

He drew her close to him, and the pure joy of feeling her body next to his was mind-spinning torture. She raised her hand and touched his face.

Turning his face, he kissed the tender side of her wrist.

"I never thought…" She stopped midsentence.

"You never thought what?"

Her laugh was short, husky and uncertain. "I never thought I'd feel like this."

"Tell me." He ran his fingers down the slender arch of her throat, and then put his mouth to the path he'd blazed.

She drew a sharp intake of breath. "Excited. Shaky. Scared."

He lifted her hand against his chest, allowing her to feel the thunderous roar inside him. "You're not alone."

Her gaze, wide and uncertain, scanned his.

He threaded his fingers through hers, pulling her hand above her head. "Tell me what you want."

Confusion puckered her forehead. "I don't know what you mean."

"Where do you want me to touch you? How fast or how slow do you want us to go?" His raspy voice reflected the strain of holding himself in check. Just being this close to her made the ache inside of him nearly unbearable. But he refused to give in to it. There would be little satisfaction if Abby's needs weren't met first.

On their wedding night, he'd allowed passion to set the pace and sweep them both away. He wouldn't allow that to happen tonight. There was more at stake. Their coming together had to be a gift for Abby. Something she could unwrap slowly, savor and relish, understanding this was hers and hers alone. No one else would be able to take this from her. Not ever. She didn't have to stand in line, or wait for hand-me-downs or castoffs. This lovemaking would be hers alone. He wanted her to claim their union and understand that no one else would push her aside. Or send her away.

She had found a home. Deep inside of him.

This is where she belonged. Forever.

Her hands fluttered against his shirt, hesitating at the buttons. "I want you to find pleasure, too."

"Your pleasure is mine." And he might die from the pure love of it.

She didn't wait for him to change his mind. Instead, she looped her hands behind his neck and pulled his mouth down to hers. Her lips brushed against his, light and uncertain at first, then passion took over and she opened her mouth and invited him inside.

Devlin fought to keep the pace even, so she wouldn't be lost and overwhelmed by the desire writhing between them. But Abby undermined his control.

Taking him at his word, her fingers attacked the buttons on his shirt and then the rest of his clothes. The details and order blurred. Devlin could only keep track of the woman in his arms. Holding her was like trying to capture a bolt of lightning. Unpredictable. Electrifying. Consuming. He wanted to cherish her, make her feel desired and special.

Yet she wouldn't hold still. Even being almost five months pregnant, she twisted around him. Her hands were everywhere. Enticing him with quicksilver caresses. Driving him crazy with their boldness.

"Slow down." The words came from his mouth before he could think.

She lifted her head, her fingers pausing. "Am I hurting you?"

"Not unless you think breathing is important."

His confession caused a dimple of mischief to dart into her cheek. "Is it?"

"What?"

"Breathing? Is it important?" With that, the little vixen nipped his earlobe.

Devlin reacted with a growl. "It's not any longer."

Then he rolled over on top of her and took control.

To heck with all his good intentions. She was determined to bring him to his knees.

The only choice she left him was to take her with him.

The call of nature woke Abby at her usual time the next morning.

Easing herself out from under Devlin's arms with great reluctance, she was rather amazed how well their bodies had curled together in spoonlike fashion even though they'd only slept together one other time. She'd slept so naturally in his arms. So trustingly. There had been a rightness she couldn't remember ever feeling before.

She left the bedside and slipped into the bathroom. When she emerged a few minutes later, she saw that Devlin was still asleep, his face now buried in her pillow.

Looking at her sleeping husband, who was still dead to the world, a curious satisfaction and warmth expanded inside of her. Even with his hair tousled by sleep and his beautiful green eyes hidden by thick lashes, he was a powerful and compelling man. She only had to recall the vivid details of their lovemaking the night before to remember the impact he had on her senses. Not once had she worried about his reaction to her bulky figure. She should have been self-conscious, but the way Devlin had touched her made her forget everything except him.

In the end, he'd given her something. He made her feel wanted.

That realization confused and frightened her. Wanting could only lead to disappointment.

She longed to climb back into bed and reclaim the place at his side before he awoke. But if she did, they'd make love again and she'd forget about why she was here and what her responsibilities were. That was a mistake she could not afford to make.

Giving one more longing glance at her husband sleeping peacefully in bed, she turned away and grabbed her robe.

Abby didn't become aware of Devlin's presence until his arms came from behind her and scooped her off the chair into his arms.

She couldn't contain the glow of warmth curling inside of her.

"What are you doing out of bed?" He nuzzled her neck, kissing the sensitive area behind her ear. "I didn't give you permission to leave, did I?"

"Since when do I need permission?"

"Since I discovered how to make you purr."

She pulled away from him and treated him to a mock frown. "You make me sound like a cat."

"You are. I've got the scratch marks to prove it." He started to reach for her again, when he caught sight of the notebook spread out on the desk. He picked it up and eyed the neat columns of numbers she'd written down. "What's this?"

"It's the notebook where I've been keeping track of my hours to pay off the debt I owe you."

A coolness chased away the warmth in his expression. His arms slackened and fell away from her. "And working on this was more important than staying in bed with me?"

"I didn't say that."

"Then what are you saying?"

She refused to let his coldness deter her. "The kids will be home soon and I wanted to finish this so I could spend more time with them." When he didn't say anything, just stood there watching her, she added, "I want to give them top priority."

She flinched as soon as the words left her mouth. "I didn't mean that the way it sounded."

His eyebrow lifted. "Really? You didn't mean that the kids and this job were more important than spending time with me?"

"You're trying to twist my meaning," she said quietly.

"Then give me a better definition." He folded his arms.

But she wasn't sure she could. Not without bungling it badly. "We agreed when we got married that my first priority would be the children. I also promised to pay back the loan. But that doesn't mean—"

"Mean what? That I'm not a priority?" He didn't wait for her answer but turned toward the door.

Then he paused and looked back at her. "What would it take to make you tear up the contract between us?"

She swallowed. "Why would I want to do that?"

"For love?"

"Love?" she echoed. Last night, he'd made her feel beautiful. Now she felt awkward and uncertain. "What does love have to do with this?"

Two strides brought him back in front of her again. "Maybe I want a real marriage where a husband and wife don't put other things like careers and money between them."

"Is that what you want?"

"I love you, Abby," he said quietly, with conviction. "That's what I want."

She stared at him helplessly, numbed by a sense of powerlessness. If she'd opened her mouth, she was afraid she'd start dribbling nonsense. Nothing in her life had prepared her for this moment. She'd been taught too well not to trust. Not to count on easy promises of love. She'd only had her own integrity. Her own personal code.

Devlin's arms clamped down on her shoulders. "Do you love me?"

The walls around her seemed to close in.

Love was fool's gold. Something that looked good on the outside but didn't have the riches inside. She'd been hurt too many times. Love was easy to dispense and just as easy to withdraw.

Voices from the ghosts of her past suddenly roared into her head.

She'd believed the Birminghams when they told her, *"As soon as Grandpa gets well and can go back to his own house, we'll send for you, Abby. You'll be our daughter."*

She'd never questioned Susie Conrad when she'd vowed, *"I'll write you every week because you're my best friend in the whole world and no one can take your place."*

She'd risked her heart and soul every time John said, *"I've got to play poker tonight, honey. Tonight's my lucky night and I'll buy you a big ring to show you how much I love you."*

She knew Devlin didn't belong to any of those voices. He was a man of his word. But she wasn't sure she knew how to love and give him what he wanted. Betrayal and rejection had deadened something inside of her.

Devlin was asking too much.

Yet she desperately wanted to slip into his arms and force the doubts and fears away. She wanted to take the chance. If it had been just her, she might have at least tried.

But what about the children?

"What about Jason, Riley, Paige and the baby?"

His mouth tightened. "What about them?"

"They're counting on us."

"Loving each other would be the best gift we could give them."

"And what if this isn't real?" She pleaded with him for assurances she knew he couldn't give her. "What if we end up disappointing each other, and end up hating each other because of that disappointment?"

"That isn't going to happen."

She shook her head impatiently. "You don't know that."

"Yes, I do."

How could she expect him to see? "I wish I had your faith, but I can't afford to. Neither of us can. Our children need two parents who will honor and respect each other. They shouldn't be at the mercy of the fickleness of love. Four innocent children are counting on us. They aren't equipped to handle our mistakes."

And neither was her heart.

Falling in love with Devlin would make her more vulnerable than she'd ever been in her life.

More than losing the love of her friend Susie, or the Birminghams' or even John's. She'd be taking the ultimate risk. Somehow, she didn't think she'd be able to recover if Devlin fell out of love with her. What would she do? How could she get through each day knowing he no longer loved her? How could she see him? How could she look at him across the dinner table? How could she sleep with him?

Her heart had been battered and bruised before. But if she risked giving Devlin her heart and he turned away from her, her heart would surely shatter into a million pieces. She knew that to be true, deep down inside to the roots of her soul.

She closed her eyes and prayed for strength before opening them again. "I want to make you happy, Devlin, but love is not something that I can trust," she said with a calmness she didn't feel. "I can only give you what I pledged to you in the contract."

She turned her back so she couldn't see the moment the love died in his eyes.

When she heard the door close quietly behind him, she let the tears fall.

Chapter Eleven

Four and a half months later, Abby had acquired a hearty sympathy for Wisconsin cows, she decided as she hoisted her bulky body out of the car after another trip to the doctor.

Awkward, trapped inside a lumpy body, supported by skinny legs, and waddling from side to side, she caught herself fighting the urge to *moo*.

Ignoring the ache in her back, she slapped at a mosquito that landed on her arm and was trying to draw her blood.

Dratted insect!

All things considered, she might be happier being a cow. At least she'd have a tail to swoosh away the mosquitoes that had hatched over the summer.

An abundance of rainy days in June had been followed by blistering heat in July, providing the ideal climate for a bumper crop of the pesky insect.

She spent more time swatting than she did anything else.

What else was there to do?

She still took care of the book work, which wasn't nearly so demanding after she'd computerized all Devlin's business records.

Since it was almost the end of August and school hadn't started yet, she didn't have to help Riley with his homework or drive Paige to preschool.

Jason had taken over all the cooking, so her presence wasn't needed or wanted in the kitchen. He'd certainly made that clear enough—especially recently.

Devlin had hired a cleaning woman to do most of the household chores. When Abby tried to protest, he'd explained that the woman needed the job and surely Abby didn't want to be responsible for depriving her of food to put on her own table.

That left Abby with too much time on her hands, time that she spent battling mosquitoes with the appetites of vampire bats.

And thinking about Devlin.

Abby leaned against the car and eyed the house in front of her, which gave her a moment to gather her inner resources before she ventured inside. Why she felt the need to brace herself, she didn't know. But sometime during the past few months, she'd begun to feel like an outsider. Everyone seemed to have a place, except her.

Paige was very content. She fought with Riley, idolized Jason and tagged along with her new daddy whenever she could. She had become a true Hamilton.

Abby was happy for her daughter, and not just a little jealous, she admitted truthfully to herself.

Rubbing her back again, Abby's thoughts drifted to Devlin and the state of their relationship.

He hadn't made love to her since that night four and

a half months ago. The closeness they'd had that weekend was no more than a memory.

They didn't argue. Their conversations were always polite and pleasant. They talked about politics, the children's activities and even the Packers' chances of going to the Super Bowl.

But they didn't cuddle or kiss, either.

Devlin went out of his way to express his appreciation and gratitude for the time she saved him with the office work. And yet, whenever she was in the study updating the records, he always left the office.

He was also very careful not to touch her. Even sharing the big bed, they didn't roll into each other during the middle of the night or curl up together.

A year ago, such an arrangement would have seemed ideal to her. But their platonic relationship didn't comfort or reassure her. Just the opposite. She felt lonely. They were doing everything according to the contract, but she was miserable.

It wasn't enough.

When they attended the Lamaze classes at the hospital, Abby had dreaded those nights as Devlin coached her through the breathing exercises, rubbed her back and touched her as if he still cared. She'd found it hard to pretend everything was normal between them. Especially in the company of all the other expectant parents who were so obviously in love and in tune with each other.

She and Devlin were existing in some kind of purgatory. There was a wall—or rather, a contract—between them, and she didn't know how to get rid of it.

Lately, he had seemed more distracted and distant. She also noticed the kids were spending more time with him and asking for his assistance instead of hers. She knew they weren't deliberately trying to shove her away, but she felt cut off nonetheless.

The worst part was this state of separation between them didn't seem to bother Devlin.

She was sure Devlin regretted that he'd ever confessed to loving her. She wished...

Wishing and having were two opposite forces. That was a reality she'd lived with all her life. There was no sense in bemoaning what couldn't be changed.

Pushing away from the car, she walked up the sidewalk.

She took a step inside the house.

"Surprise!" The chorus of cheers inside the dining room brought Abby to a complete stop.

Her jaw dropped open as she eyed the scene in front of her. Riley, Paige and Kelly Castner crowded around a brightly decorated birthday cake that was topped with enough candles to start a forest fire. On the opposite side of the room, Jason was trying to hold up the streamers that were beginning to come loose from the chandelier as Rebecca and Cash came to his assistance. Only Devlin stood apart, watching her.

"Happy Birthday, Mommy." Paige clapped her hands, excitement dancing from her blue eyes. "We're giving you a party with lots and lots of presents."

"Open mine first," Riley demanded as he pushed a gift toward her.

Devlin pulled out a chair and settled her in it. Before he moved away, she grabbed his arm. "You planned this?" She still was having trouble accepting the notion that this party was for her, and why. Did that mean he still cared for her? That he might still love her?

"The kids helped."

"How did you know it was my birthday?"

For the first time in weeks, his face gave way to a grin. 'I peeked at your driver's license.''

Riley shook his present in front of her face. "Open it.''

She took the package that seemed to have more tape than wrapping.

Rebecca sat down next to her and handed her scissors. "You didn't have a clue, did you?''

Abby shook her head. "I had no idea.''

"Then your head must have been in another planet because they've been whispering and talking about it for weeks. I thought Devlin was going to throttle them all.''

Abby snipped the tape and looked at Devlin from the corner of her eye. He had done this for her even though she'd told him that she couldn't love him. Why? Her backache grew more pronounced as she pried open the box and pulled out a baseball glove.

"How did you know I wanted a baseball glove?'' she asked the beaming boy at her side.

"I guessed.'' He grinned, exposing a gap of spaces where his teeth were supposed to be. "Now we can play catch together.''

"I'd like that.''

"And me and Jason can baby-sit the baby,'' Paige added, tucking her small hand into Jason's.

"That's quite a deal,'' Cash drawled. "I'd get it in writing, Abby.''

"Just don't expect me to change any diapers.'' Jason scowled, but he didn't pull away from Paige's grip.

Over their heads, Devlin's gaze met Abby's and she saw a hint of laughter in the jade depths. Her heart warmed.

Jason gave her a sweatshirt picturing a giant mosquito and a caption that read, Wisconsin's State Bird. Paige had drawn her a picture and gave her a miniature tea set. Abby was particularly touched by the beautiful water-color of a gazebo that Rebecca had painted for her.

When she thanked her, Rebecca said, "I loved doing it. I could shut out Cash reading me the sports page."

"Hey, I heard that," Cash said as all the adults in the room chuckled.

The final gift that Abby opened was from Devlin.

The stark white box was accented by a big gold bow and matching ribbon. Her fingers trembled as she care-fully pulled back the paper and opened the box that bore the name of an exclusive women's clothing store. Inside she found an exquisite tunic-style lounging outfit. Abby struggled to hold back the tears as she lifted the royal-blue garment and held it up for everyone to see.

"It's beautiful." She tried to hold her smile steady but found the effort almost more than she could manage as she met Devlin's gaze.

She saw the satisfaction—and something else—in his expression before Riley grabbed his arm. "Dad, can we eat now?"

When Devlin turned away to attend to the food, Abby was left with more questions than answers. And a strange feeling of hope. Cash and Devlin insisted that she and Rebecca sit and chat while the two men dished up the cake and ice cream. The kids passed out the dishes before sitting down to devour their own desserts.

Rebecca and Cash didn't stay long afterward. As soon as they left, Abby helped Paige get ready for bed. The excitement had worn off and Paige was half-asleep by the time Abby tucked her in.

Her daughter lifted her head. "I want Daddy to give me a good-night kiss."

Abby moved aside as Devlin came into the room and bent low to give Paige a loud smack and a bear hug.

Paige giggled. "I love you, Daddy."

He tweaked her nose lightly. "I love you, honey." He made the words sound so natural and effortless, as if they were statements of fact. Maybe they were.

Abby looked away and left the room.

Devlin joined her a few minutes later in the living room. "I think she was asleep before I closed the door."

Abby shook her head in amazement. "It must have taken a lot of energy to keep her from giving away that secret."

Devlin's mouth twisted into a wry grimace. "You don't know the half of it. I finally told Jason to keep the two younger ones away from you as much as possible so they couldn't spill the beans."

She realized the signs were there that something was definitely going on, but she'd been too busy trying to analyze the situation with Devlin to pay much heed to the mystery surrounding the children's behavior. "You went to a lot of trouble."

"Some things are worth it."

"Are they?" She searched his face, trying to read his expression. There was an aura of waiting hovering around him, as if he was looking for something. A signal from her, perhaps? "Was planning the party worth it for you?"

He didn't answer right away. Finally, he said, "I've been trying to stick to the terms we set in our contract, Abby. I've done everything in my power to give you the space you need. But I'm not sure I can do that anymore."

Did that mean he wanted her to leave? That he wanted to end this marriage? She licked her lips and tried not to give in to the fear shooting through her. "Do you want a divorce? Is that what you want, because if you do—"

"No, I don't want a divorce." He moved close to her and reached for her hands, his grip nearly cutting off her circulation. "I don't want your damn money. I don't care if you wash my clothes or darn my socks. I don't care if you can't cook anything but an egg. I didn't marry you for any of those reasons."

"You married me because of Riley and Jason."

"No." His gaze held hers.

"No?"

"I married you for me. For no other reason. I put together that stupid contract so I could have you for me."

"You did?" The word was barely a whisper.

He pulled her close to him, his hands so light that she could have pulled away if she'd wanted to. And when she didn't, he lowered his head, his gaze full of intent, never leaving hers for a moment. Then his lips touched hers, gently, coaxingly, and her eyes drifted shut. The kiss was earth-shatteringly sweet. And devastatingly brief. She started to open her mouth when he ended it.

Dragging open her heavy eyelids, her gaze caught the blazing demand in his. His hands tightened on her shoulders. "I know you don't believe in love. I know you're afraid to trust me, but that doesn't change anything." His low-pitched voice rang with meaning. "I love you, Abby, and that's never going to change. I want to tear up that stupid contract and have a real marriage. A real relationship. All I'm asking for is a chance to prove to you that we've got something more than four children and a contract between us."

The air sizzled between them.

Every part of Abby's being hurt. She'd been alone

most of her life. And she was tired of it. She was tired of trying to be strong. She was tired of being afraid.

She hurt emotionally and physically. All her happiness rested in Devlin.

She loved him. She realized that now. But did she love him enough to risk tearing up the contract and letting the marriage take its full course?

Before she could make the decision, the pronounced ache in her back became sharper. Her hands cupped her stomach.

"Devlin?" His name came out as a gasp.

Immediately he reached for her. "What is it? What's the matter?"

She looked up at him helplessly. "We're going to have a baby."

Chapter Twelve

Devlin took one look at Abby and, without saying a word, he swept her into his arms and headed toward the door.

"I can walk."

He ignored her protest as he carried her to the car and set her inside. "I'll be right back." He shut the door and raced up the front steps.

Then he was back.

"What about the kids?" she asked after he'd gotten behind the wheel and started the engine.

"They're fine. I told Jason we were going, and I called my parents. They're coming over right away."

"Devlin, I wanted to tell you—"

"Don't worry about it now, it's not important."

This time she wouldn't cower and run. "But I need to—" Another contraction broadsided her, cutting her off.

Devlin floored the accelerator as his right hand covered

hers, his strength reaching out to her. "No explanations. Just hold on to me."

She didn't have much choice except to do exactly what he suggested. With the beginning of the next contraction, she gave up the fight to talk and hung on for all she was worth, grateful for the steadiness and strength Devlin gave her.

By the time she got to the hospital, the contractions were less than two minutes apart. Everything around her blurred.

Her only reality was Devlin.

He didn't leave her side for a moment, even when the nurse tried to brush him aside. "I'm staying." His inflexible growl didn't brook any arguments. The nurse quit trying to shoo him away while the doctor examined her.

From then on, things happened so fast, Abby wasn't conscious of anything except that she wouldn't have made it through without Devlin at her side. He became her rock, her anchor, smoothing her hair and wiping her forehead with a cool cloth.

Inside the delivery room, Devlin coached her with ruthless determination. She breathed when he said, "Breathe" and panted when he said, "Pant."

Then came the welcome sound she'd been straining to hear. A baby's cry at the same time the doctor announced, "It's a girl. A real beauty."

Relief and emotion rushed over Abby.

"Does she have all her toes and fingers?" she asked Devlin.

"Want to see?"

At her exhausted nod, Devlin slid his hands under her head and lifted.

Red-faced, and squirming her outrage for being

wrested from her sanctuary, her new daughter was letting everyone know she wasn't pleased.

The doctor chuckled through his mask. "Everything's accounted for, including a set of high-powered lungs."

Abby sank back and met Devlin's gaze. She saw the hint of moisture there. Smiling tremulously, she said, "She's beautiful, isn't she?"

"Almost as beautiful as her mother."

The heartfelt emotion behind his words brought tears to her eyes.

Abby woke in her hospital bed a few hours later to hear Devlin's voice crooning softly in the background.

"You're going to be a real heartbreaker like your mother. I can see that already." The husky timbre to his voice couldn't hide the wonder. "Stubborn. Independent. With a heart as big as the outdoors. I'll have to beat off the boys with a baseball bat and lock you in a tower."

Abby raised her eyelids and saw Devlin standing next to the window, talking to the bundle in his arms. If she hadn't realized she loved him before, Abby would have fallen head over heels in love with her husband right at this very moment. With his face just inches from the baby in his arms, he was giving her his first father-to-daughter talk.

Whether the baby was asleep or hypnotized by the sound of her father's voice, Abby couldn't determine. What she did recognize was the steadfast feeling in her husband's voice.

The sheer power of his love filled the room.

Abby wouldn't doubt one bit that Devlin would do bodily harm to anyone who messed with his daughter. Or with any of his kids, for that matter. He was a man whose word and promises could be counted on. He would always be there for their daughter, just as he was there for Jason, Riley and Paige. Devoted. He was a man whose commitment was solid. Unshakable. Devlin was the type of man who would never put his own needs before his family's.

All during the delivery, he'd been right there, his hand steady and sure. So different from John who had fainted before Paige had been born.

Her husband was a man she could trust. He wouldn't ever turn away from his family or give up when times got tough.

Their baby might not know it yet, but she was the luckiest baby in the world to have Devlin for a father.

Devlin lifted his head and grinned at Abby. He'd known she was listening because she had a tendency to twitch her foot when she was awake. He'd learned this habit after months of trying to sleep next to her and not being able to touch her. Sleep had been next to impossible. Instead, he'd memorized the sound of her breathing, the little whispering sounds she made and the curve of her body against the sheets. There wasn't much he didn't know about his wife or her habits.

Except how she felt about him.

But he had patience, time and a lot of hope. Sometime during the hours they'd spent together bringing their baby into the world, a few home truths had finally knocked some sense into his brain. He'd been a fool to reject Abby's attempt to pay back the money she wanted to give him. It was true he didn't need or want the money, but to Abby she was giving him every cent she had. It was a sign of her commitment to their marriage. To their family. To him. Why hadn't he realized that? She was sharing everything she had to give.

He'd been a fool not to realize it sooner.

He knew it now. That meant he could set things right. If she'd give him the chance to make it up to her.

He left his perch next to the window and walked toward Abby, while still talking to the baby. "Look who's awake, little one. It's your mommy." He settled on the bed next to Abby and placed the baby in her arms.

The smile that came naturally to Abby's face as she looked down at their daughter made Devlin's heart thunder so loud he thought the whole world would hear it. He'd been waiting for her to wake up. Not just so they could talk, but because he wanted to be with her. To share this time between the two of them and their daughter.

She ran a finger along the baby's smooth face. "She looks a lot like Riley, don't you think?"

"She sure bellows like he did."

She looked up at him. "Did you go home?"

He nodded. "Cash is going to bring the kids by later."

"What did they say when you told them about the baby?"

"Jason pretended to act indifferent. Riley wanted to know if he could hold the baby first. And Paige asked if she could take the baby to preschool for show-and-tell."

She laughed but there were tears in her eyes, too. She looked down at the baby and then back up at him. "Thank you."

"For what?"

"I never thought I'd ever find this kind of happiness."

Before he could say anything, she surprised him by shifting the baby to one arm and reaching up to kiss him softly on the side of the mouth.

When she lifted her head, her heart shone from her eyes. "I love you. I'm sorry I was such a coward and didn't tell you before."

A powerful emotion slammed into his midsection. He didn't need to hear any more. That Abby loved him was the only thing that mattered. Emotion rushed through him.

He reached over and drew her back to him. This time he put all his feelings for her into the kiss.

Giving.

Receiving.

And making promises that would last forever.

"Ah, heck." Jason's voice, thick with teenage disgust, sounded from the doorway. "They're locking lips."

With rich satisfaction flowing through him, Devlin released Abby slowly and grinned at her. "I think our other children have arrived."

He watched their three oldest children come into the room, Jason hanging to the back while Riley and Paige raced immediately to the bed.

"Can I hold the baby first?" Riley asked.

As Abby helped him get into position so he could hold the baby, Paige tugged Devlin's leg. "Daddy, I can't see my baby."

He hoisted Paige onto the bed so she could get a better look.

"What's her name?" Paige asked.

"We haven't chosen one yet," her mother said.

"Can we call her Molly?" Riley said. "That's a nice name."

Jason produced a snort and drifted closer to the bed. "That's because you like Molly Smythe. Last week you wanted to *marry* Beth Everett. We can't change her name every time a girl dumps you."

Devlin noticed that Abby made a valiant effort to keep her humor from showing. Instead, she turned toward Jason, who was trying to pretend he had no interest in the baby. "Jason, what name do you like?"

He shrugged. At that moment, the baby opened her eyes and blinked at him. He put his finger next to her hand and tried not to look too pleased when her tiny fist wrapped around him. "Angela is cool, I guess."

Paige crowded closer. "I like Angela, too."

"Me, too," Riley added.

Abby's gaze rose to meet Devlin's. "What do you think?"

"I'd say it's unanimous," he said.

Two months later, Devlin came home to find the house empty. The only light seemed to be the one coming from the living room.

"Abby?"

"In here," came the reply.

He tossed down the keys on the counter and walked through the kitchen to the living room.

His wife was standing with her back to him, trying to start a fire.

He frowned. "Let me do that."

She stepped back and handed him the matches. Within a few minutes, the flames began to eat up the wood, casting a rosy glow to the room. Turning around, he saw Abby was dressed in the satin lounging outfit he'd given her for her birthday. Need stampeded through him. It had been too many months since he'd made love to his wife.

"Where are the kids?" he asked.

"Angela's just been fed and should sleep for a couple of hours. Jason's staying at a friend's house. And Riley and Paige are spending the night at Cash and Rebecca's."

"Just the two of us for a couple of hours?" He tossed off his jacket. "I wonder what we should do."

"I've got a few ideas."

"Such as?"

She reached behind her and pulled out a file folder. "I thought we might want to officially get rid of this contract."

He took it from her hand. "No regrets?"

"None."

He leaned down and fed the paper to the flames. As he slipped his arm around his wife's shoulders, she said, "I have a gift for you."

"If it's what you're wearing under that pajama thing, I can't wait to start unwrapping it."

She laughed, a tinkling sexy sound that made his body snap to attention. "That's your other present." She went over to the end table and picked up a thick envelope.

He took it but made no move to open it. "What is it?"

A mysterious, seductive smile chased across her lips. "Open it and you'll find out."

It was the smile that did it. Curiosity got the better of him and he flipped up the flap. Inside, he found five bank-account passbooks. Opening them one by one, he discovered that each one bore the name of one of their children and contained an equal amount of money. He looked up at her. "You started savings accounts for the kids?"

"I took the money from the sale of the house in Cincinnati and opened college accounts for each one."

He lifted the cover of the fifth book, which was identified as the A & D account. "What's this one for?"

"It stands for the Abby & Devlin account," she explained. "I don't know if we'll have any more children or not. But in case we do, I didn't want him or her to be left with nothing. I wanted all the kids to be treated equally."

Abby's soft heart couldn't bear the thought of another

child being caught on the outside looking in. Not the way she had been.

The fact that she'd treated the boys as equally as she'd treated the girls brought a fullness to his chest. She had taken his children to her heart and accepted them as hers. But Abby being Abby, he wouldn't have expected anything different.

"You approve?" she asked.

He didn't really care what happened to the money. She could do whatever she wanted with it. It was the love they had for each other that was important. It was a love that grew each day and was fulfilled through their family as well as themselves.

He set down the envelope and opened his arms. "It's perfect, and so are you."

Abby walked into them without an ounce of hesitation. "Now do I get to open my other present?" he asked, his fingers already starting to unfasten the buttons of her fancy pajamas.

She laughed, a sound that was both seductive and teasing. "We could always look at those whirlpool brochures again and review your floor plans for our new bathroom, if you'd like."

"Later. My top priority is to make love to my wife." He lifted her into his arms. "Any objections?"

Abby offered her face to him and he saw all the love and trust he'd ever hoped for. "Not a single one."

* * * * *

Bestselling author

JOAN JOHNSTON

continues her wildly popular miniseries with an
all-new, longer-length novel

The Virgin Groom

HAWK'S WAY

One minute, Mac Macready was a living legend in
Texas—every kid's idol, every man's envy, every
woman's fantasy. The next, his fiancée dumped him,
his career was hanging in the balance and his future
was looking mighty uncertain. Then there was the
matter of his scandalous secret, which didn't stand a
chance of staying a secret. So would he succumb to
Jewel Whitelaw's shocking proposal—or take cold
showers for the rest of the long, hot summer...?

Available August 1997
wherever Silhouette books are sold.

▼ *Silhouette*®
™

Take 4 bestselling love stories FREE

Plus get a FREE surprise gift!

Special Limited-time Offer

Mail to Silhouette Reader Service™

3010 Walden Avenue
P.O. Box 1867
Buffalo, N.Y. 14240-1867

YES! Please send me 4 free Silhouette Romance™ novels and my free surprise gift. Then send me 6 brand-new novels every month, which I will receive months before they appear in bookstores. Bill me at the low price of $2.67 each plus 25¢ delivery and applicable sales tax, if any.* That's the complete price and a savings of over 10% off the cover prices—quite a bargain! I understand that accepting the books and gift places me under no obligation ever to buy any books. I can always return a shipment and cancel at any time. Even if I never buy another book from Silhouette, the 4 free books and the surprise gift are mine to keep forever.

215 BPA A3UT

Name	(PLEASE PRINT)	
Address		Apt. No.
City	State	Zip

This offer is limited to one order per household and not valid to present Silhouette Romance™ subscribers. *Terms and prices are subject to change without notice. Sales tax applicable in N.Y.

USROM-696   ©1990 Harlequin Enterprises Limited

Wanted: Brides! This small South Dakota town
needs women of marriageable age. And
Silhouette Romance invites you to visit the
handsome, extremely eligible men of:

Bachelor
Gulch

a new miniseries by
Sandra Steffen

♥ The local veterinarian finds himself falling for his feisty
receptionist—the one woman in town *not* interested in
finding herself a husband.

LUKE'S WOULD-BE BRIDE
(June '97)

♥ This sheriff's got a reputation for being the good guy, yet a
certain single gal has him wanting to prove just what a wolf in
sheep's clothing he really is.

WYATT'S MOST WANTED WIFE
(August '97)

♥ A rugged rancher proposes a marriage of convenience to a
dowdy diner waitress, but just wait till his ugly-duckling
bride turns into a swan.

CLAYTON'S MADE-OVER MRS.
(October '97)

Don't miss any of these wonderful love stories, available only from

V Silhouette ROMANCE™

Silhouette ROMANCE™

COMING NEXT MONTH

#1240 BABY BUSINESS—Laura Anthony

Bundles of Joy

Caring for infants was business as usual to lovely pediatrician Tobie Avery, but when millionaire bachelor Clay Barton asked for her help, Tobie wondered if the baby's rugged uncle would consider her for a more permanent position—as his wife!

#1241 WYATT'S MOST WANTED WIFE—Sandra Steffen

Bachelor Gulch

Lisa Markman came to Jasper Gulch looking for a husband and a new life. But Sheriff Wyatt McCully, a man with a reputation as sterling as his badge, *wasn't* the man for her, no matter how sexy or intriguing he was! Especially if the handsome lawman found out about the past she was fleeing....

#1242 MARRY IN HASTE—Moyra Tarling

Jade had never forgotten the man who had pledged her his heart, and then torn it away. Now devastatingly handsome Evan Mathieson had returned, and was asking once again for her hand in marriage. But could Jade trust their love a second time, when she harbored a terrible secret that touched them both?

#1243 HUSBAND IN RED—Cara Colter

Sadie McGee was back home to care for her family. Romance was *not* in her plans. But Michael O'Bryan, the town's golden boy, had never forgotten the sexy girl from the wrong side of the tracks—and would win her back no matter what....

#1244 THE RAINBOW BRIDE—Elizabeth Sites

A Western wedding? Pretty librarian Iris Merlin came to the old town of Felicity looking for answers to her family's scandalous past, not love! But rugged Adam Freemont soon captured her passion, and had Iris dreaming of becoming the gorgeous man's wife.

#1245 MARRIAGE IS JUST THE BEGINNING— Betty Jane Sanders

To keep his little girl, single father Grant Parker would gladly marry the lovely Sharon O'Riley—in name only. After all, Sharon had known little Cassie since birth, and treated her as her own. But this caring, warm beauty also had other charms, and Grant soon suspected that marriage to Sharon was just the beginning....